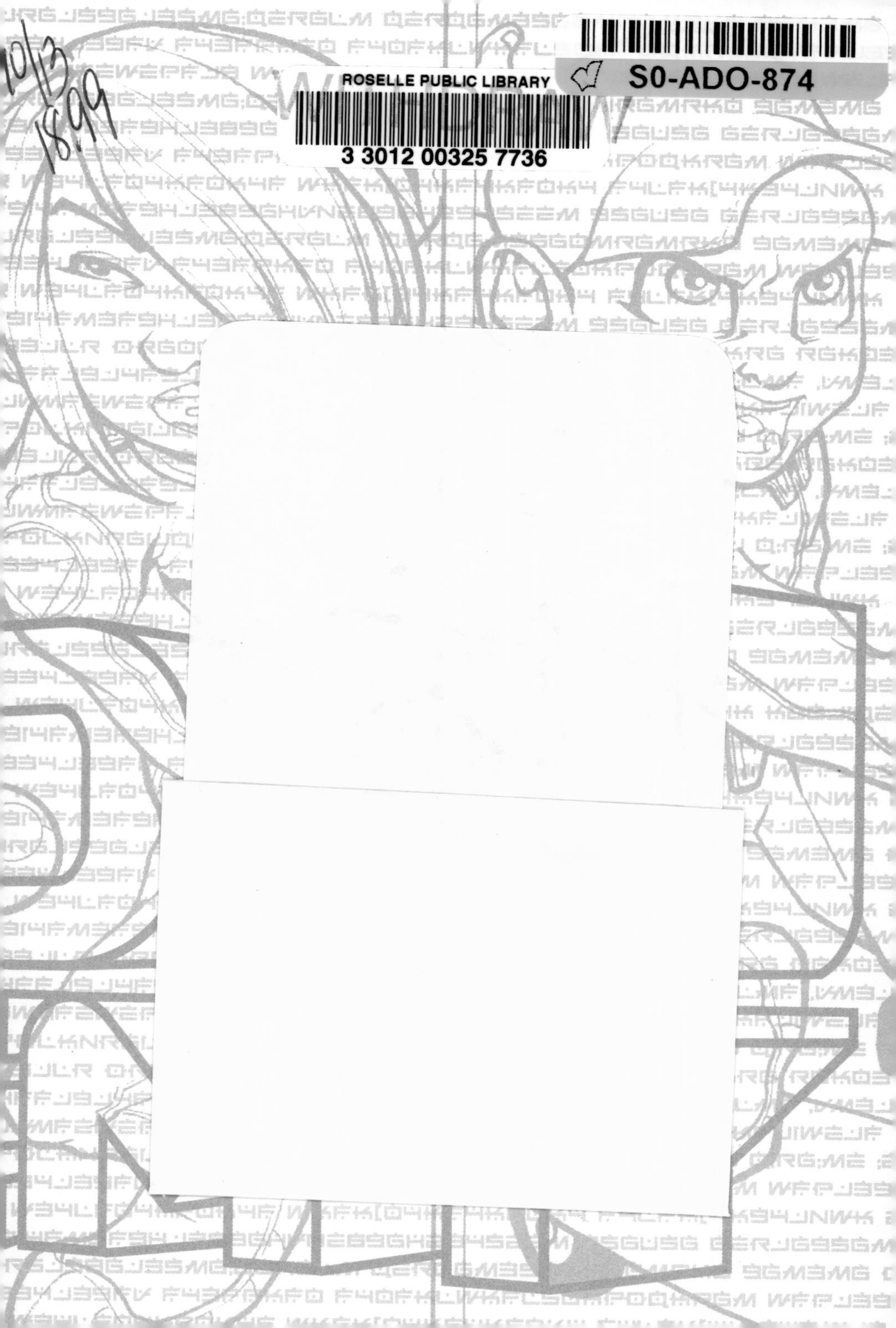

10/13
18.99

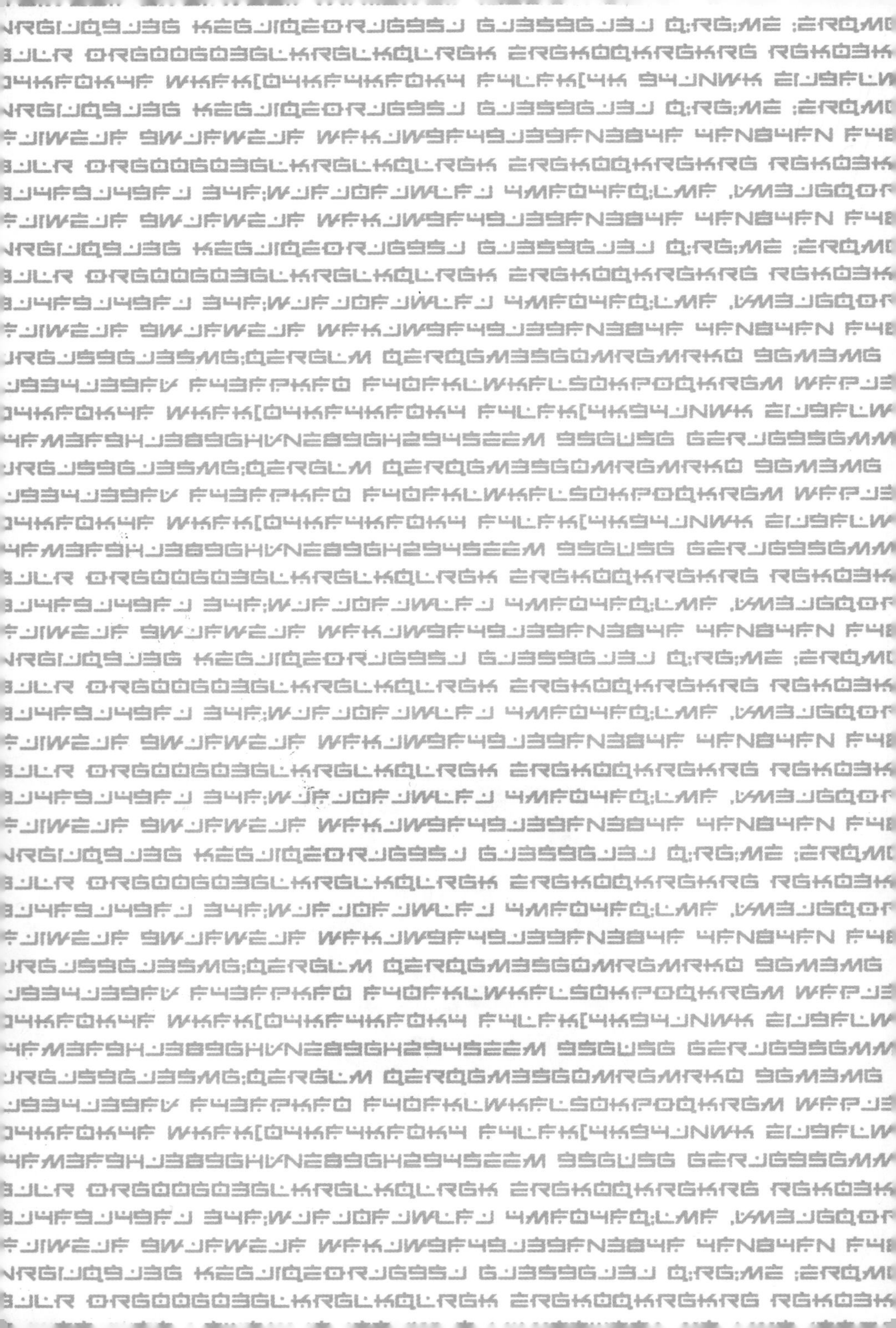

RECON ACADEMY

DEMOLITION DAY

BY CHRIS EVERHEART
ILLUSTRATED BY ARCANA STUDIO

ACCESS GRANTED >>>>

STONE ARCH BOOKS
a capstone imprint

Recon Academy is published by Stone Arch Books
A Capstone Imprint
151 Good Counsel Drive, P.O. Box 669
Mankato, Minnesota 56002
www.capstonepub.com

Cataloging-in-Publication Data is available on the Library of Congress
website.

Library binding: 978-1-4342-1917-6

Summary: The U.S. Navy asks Recon Academy to tighten their security
during an important building demolition, and the teens are eager to accept.
After all, what's cooler than zooming around the desert in dune buggies
while watching a giant building explode? But soon, a strange vehicle
pops up on the horizon, and the Navy asks Recon to investigate. As they
approach the truck, it suddenly disappears! When the team tries to track
down the missing vehicle, they discover that Shadow Cell is behind the
plot, and they're after the Navy's top-secret documents!

Designer: Brann Garvey
Art Director: Bob Lentz
Production Specialist: Michelle Biedscheid
Series Editor: Donnie Lemke
Series Concept: Michael Dahl, Brann Garvey, Heather Kindseth,
    Donnie Lemke

Printed in the United States of America in Stevens Point, Wisconsin.
092009
005619WZS10

TABLE OF CONTENTS

>>>> ENTER

 > GADGETRY

 > MARTIAL ARTS

 > COMPUTERS

 > FORENSICS

TEAM BREAKDOWN

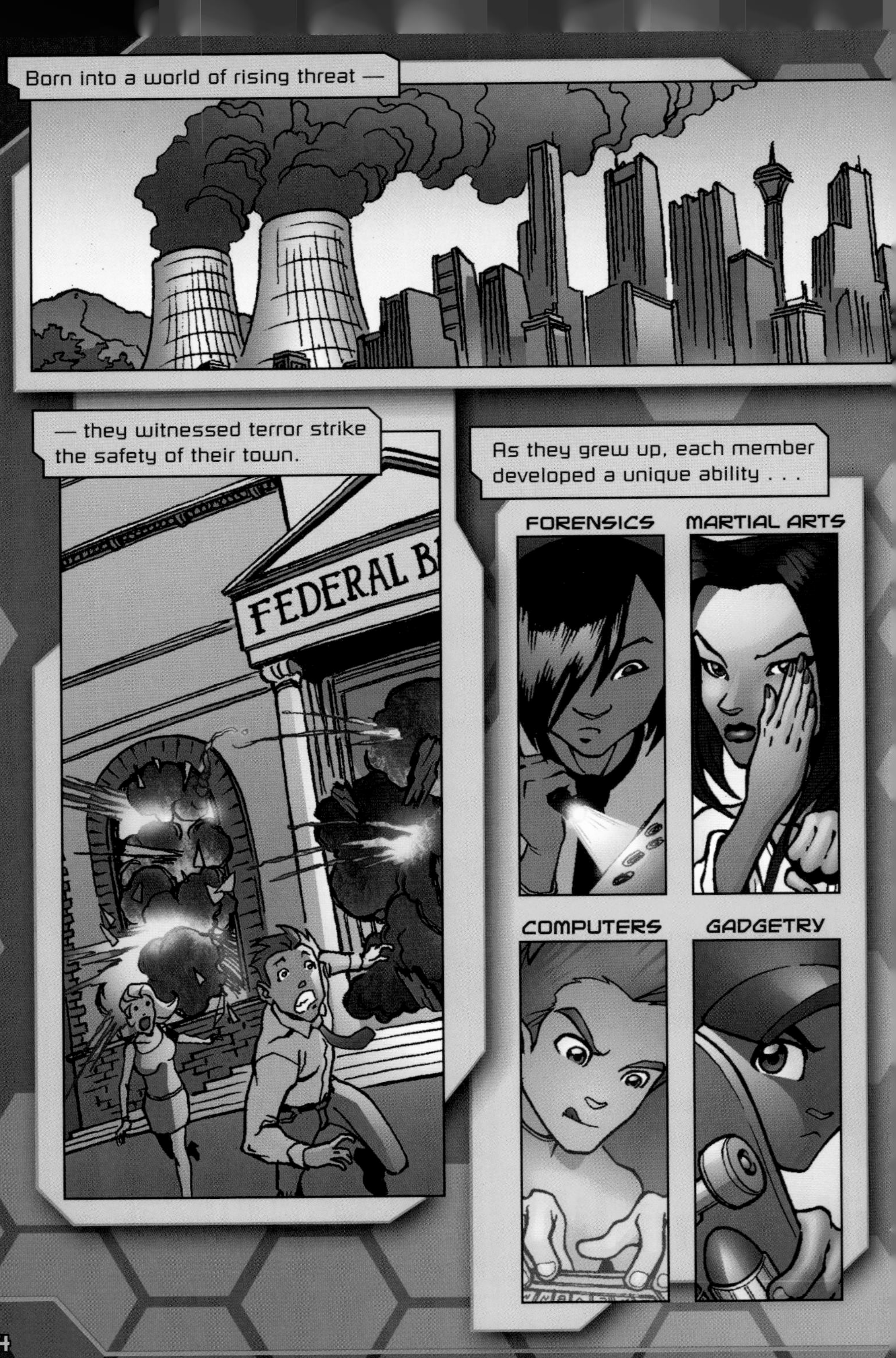
Born into a world of rising threat —
— they witnessed terror strike the safety of their town.
FEDERAL B
As they grew up, each member developed a unique ability . . .
FORENSICS
MARTIAL ARTS
COMPUTERS
GADGETRY

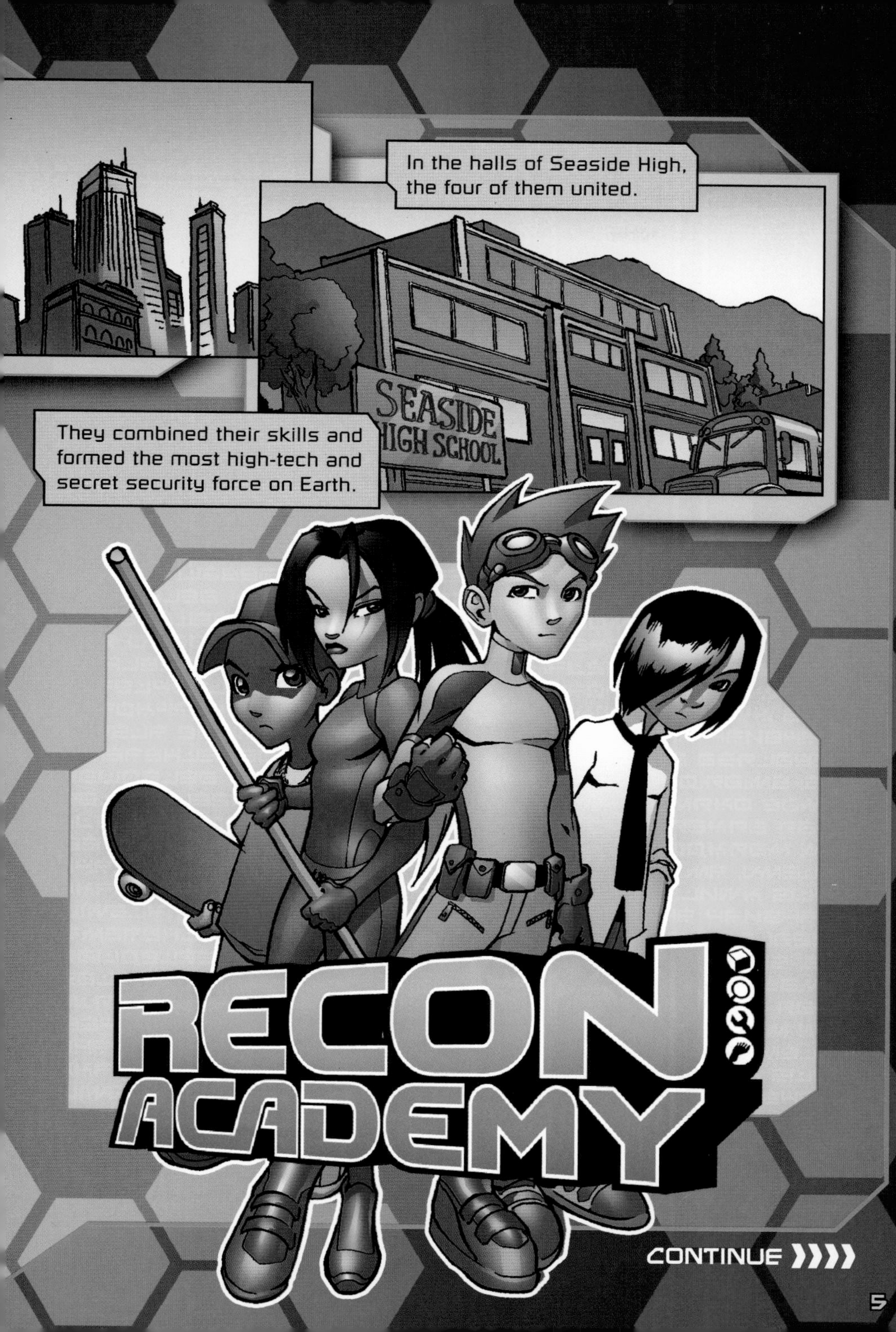
In the halls of Seaside High, the four of them united.
SEASIDE HIGH SCHOOL
They combined their skills and formed the most high-tech and secret security force on Earth.
RECON ACADEMY
CONTINUE

SECTION

1

ACCESS GRANTED)))⟩

RECON ACADEMY
SECRET SECURITY FORCE

128718
293829
9283
98289
89
1
109201
192091
1992

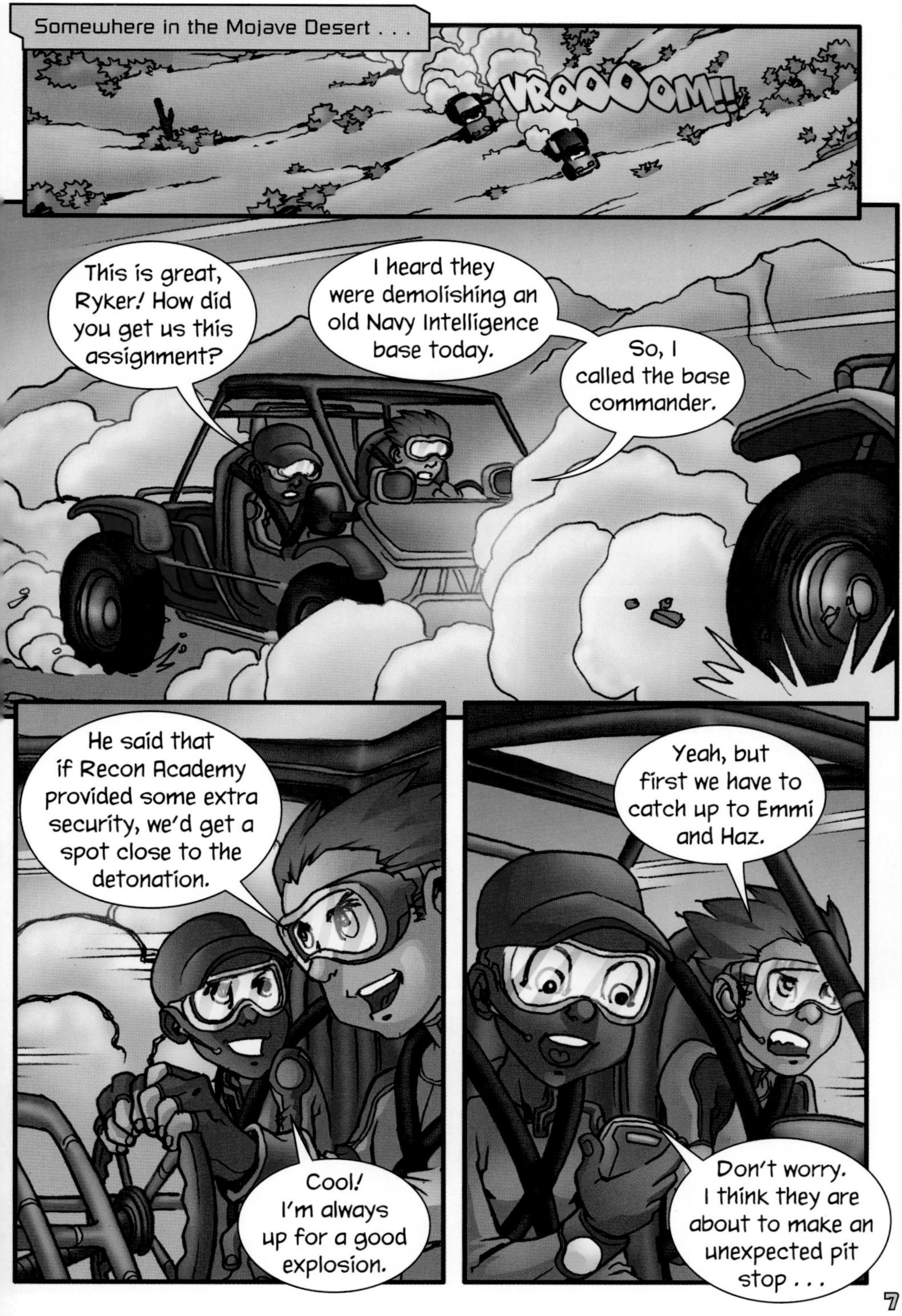
Somewhere in the Mojave Desert . . .
VROOOOOM!!
This is great, Ryker! How did you get us this assignment?
I heard they were demolishing an old Navy Intelligence base today.
So, I called the base commander.
He said that if Recon Academy provided some extra security, we'd get a spot close to the detonation.
Cool! I'm always up for a good explosion.
Yeah, but first we have to catch up to Emmi and Haz.
Don't worry. I think they are about to make an unexpected pit stop . . .

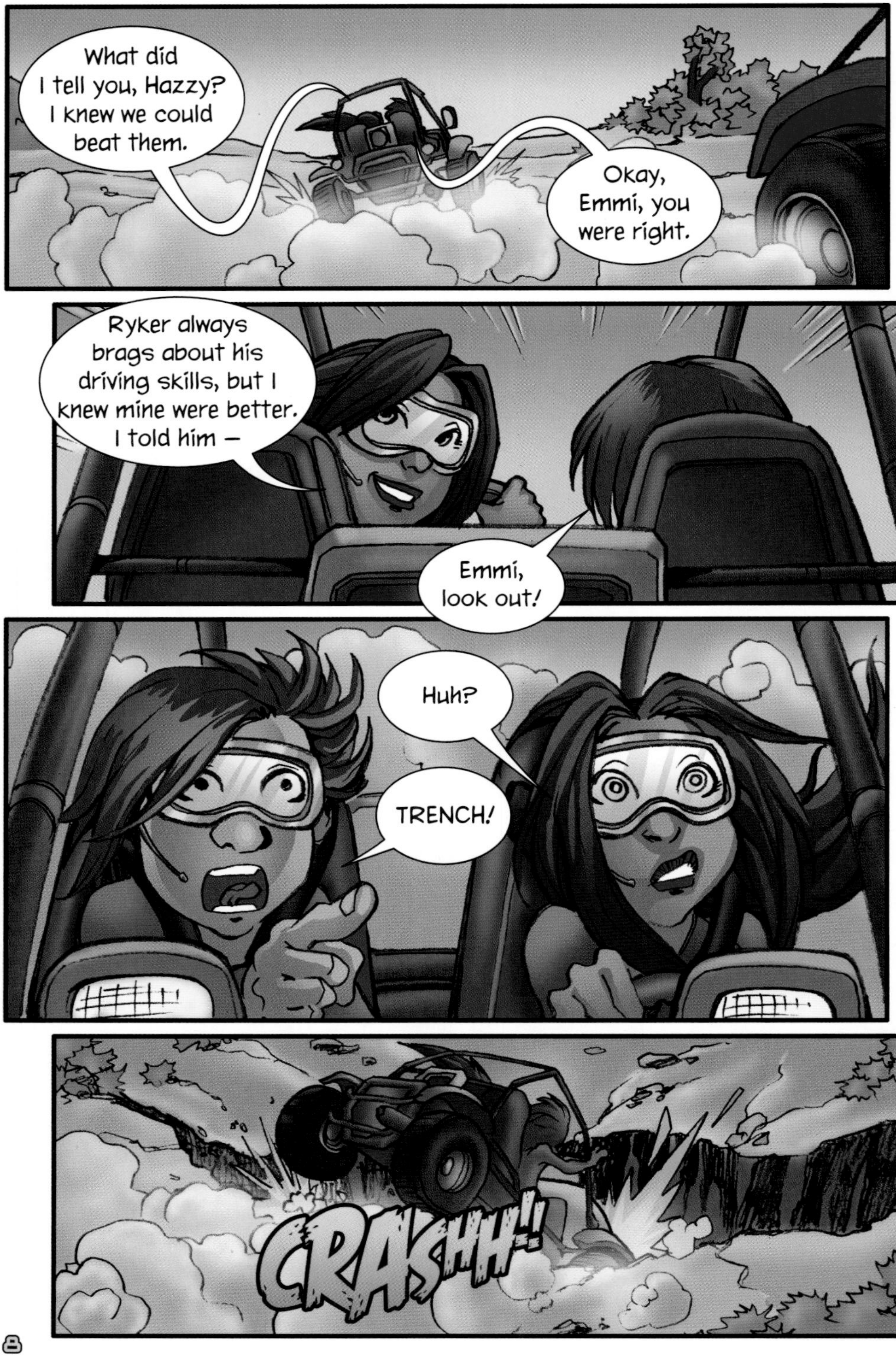
What did I tell you, Hazzy? I knew we could beat them.
Okay, Emmi, you were right.
Ryker always brags about his driving skills, but I knew mine were better. I told him —
Emmi, look out!
Huh?
TRENCH!
CRASHH!!

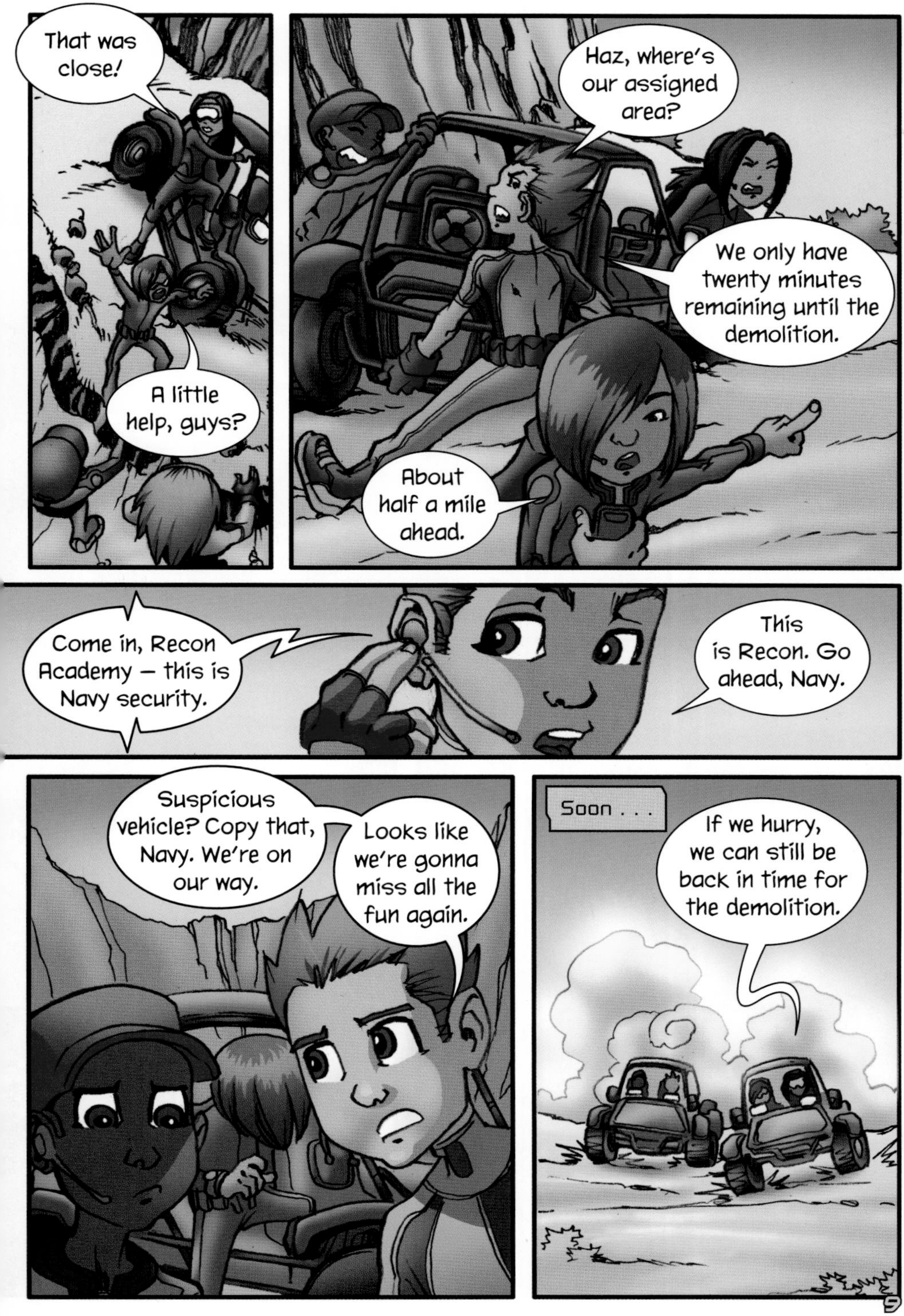

That was close!
A little help, guys?
Haz, where's our assigned area?
We only have twenty minutes remaining until the demolition.
About half a mile ahead.
Come in, Recon Academy — this is Navy security.
This is Recon. Go ahead, Navy.
Suspicious vehicle? Copy that, Navy. We're on our way.
Looks like we're gonna miss all the fun again.
Soon . . .
If we hurry, we can still be back in time for the demolition.

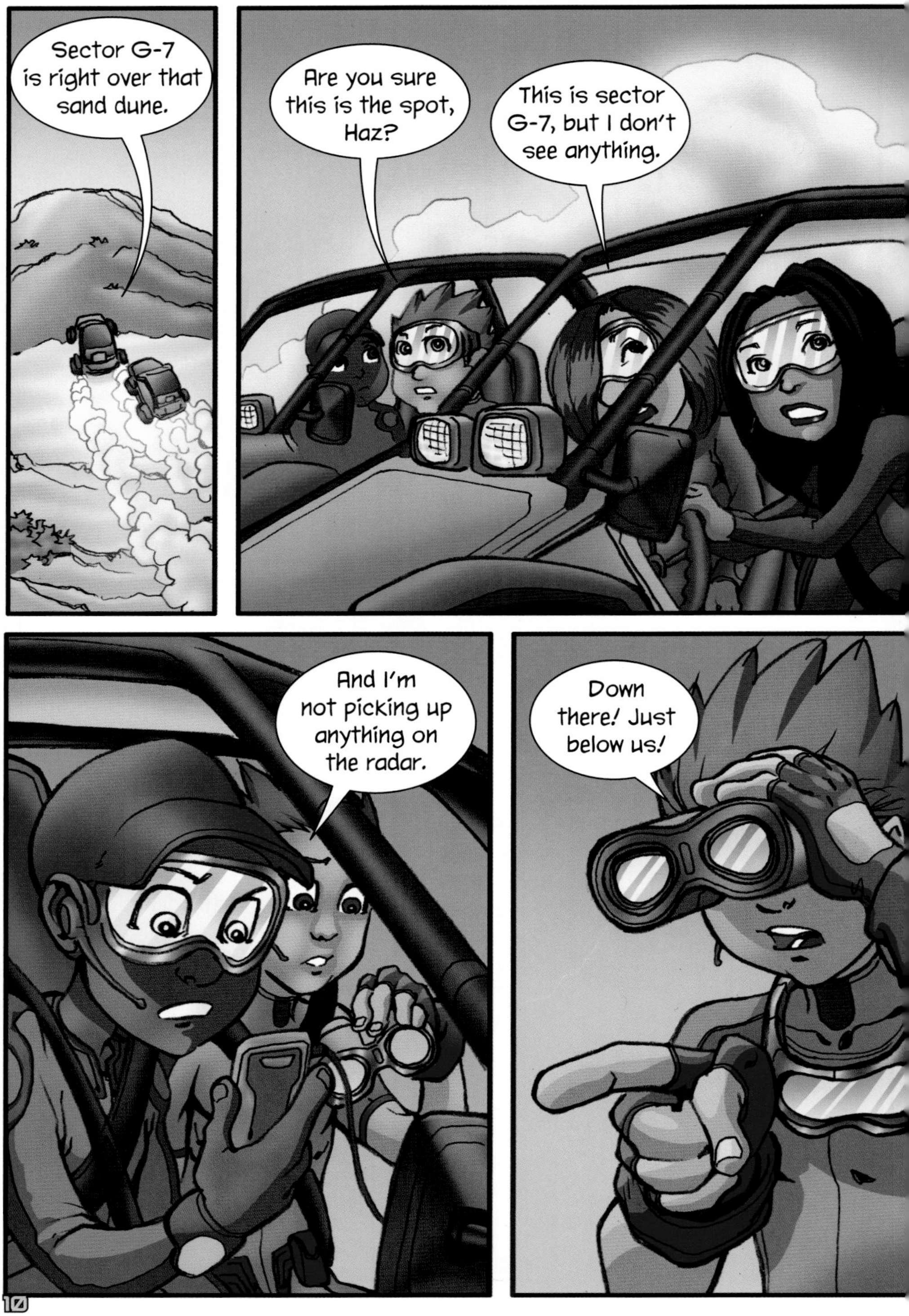
Sector G-7 is right over that sand dune.
Are you sure this is the spot, Haz?
This is sector G-7, but I don't see anything.
And I'm not picking up anything on the radar.
Down there! Just below us!

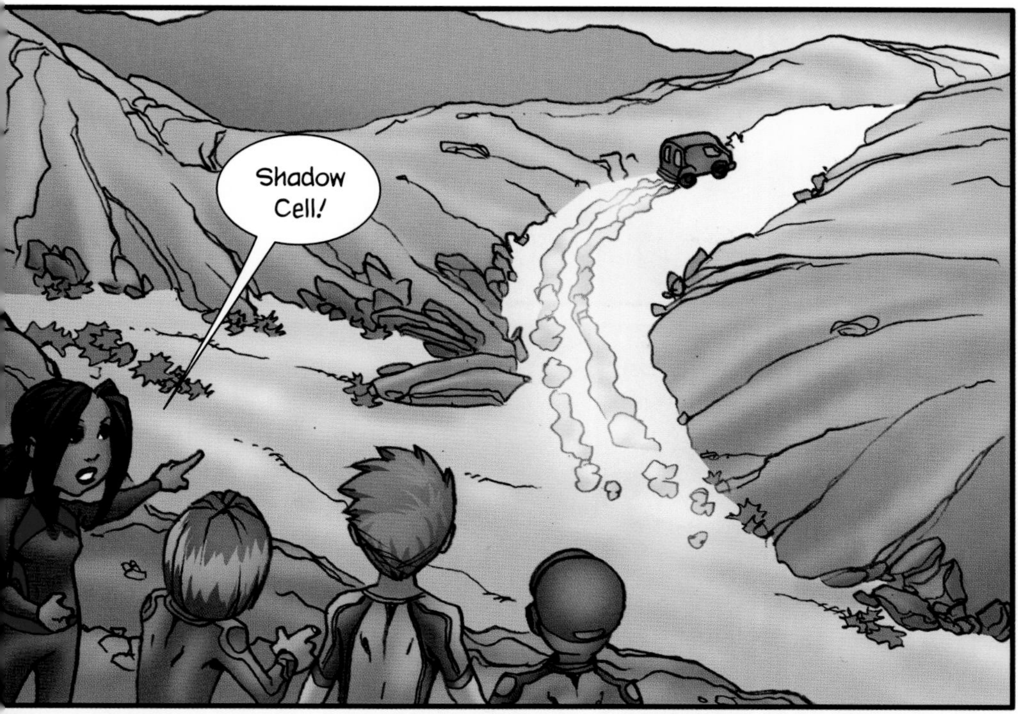
Shadow Cell!
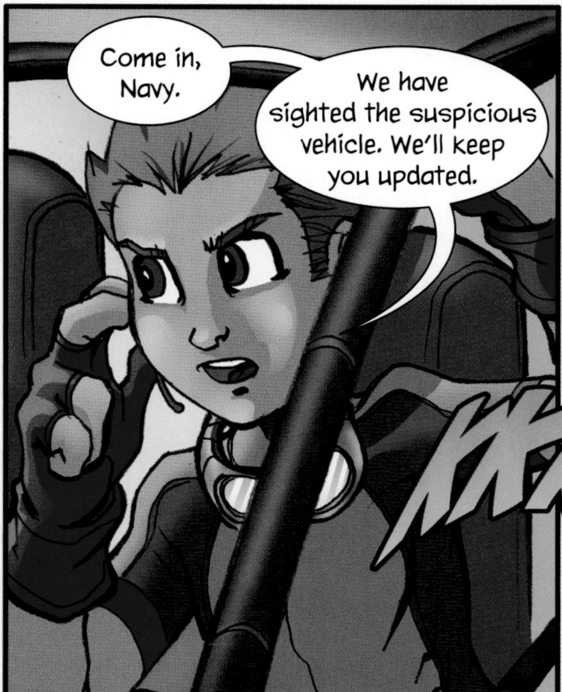
Come in, Navy.
We have sighted the suspicious vehicle. We'll keep you updated.
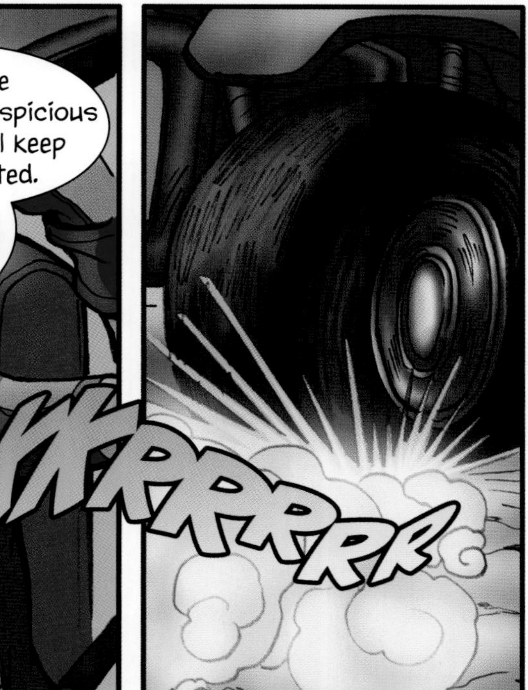
WRRRRR

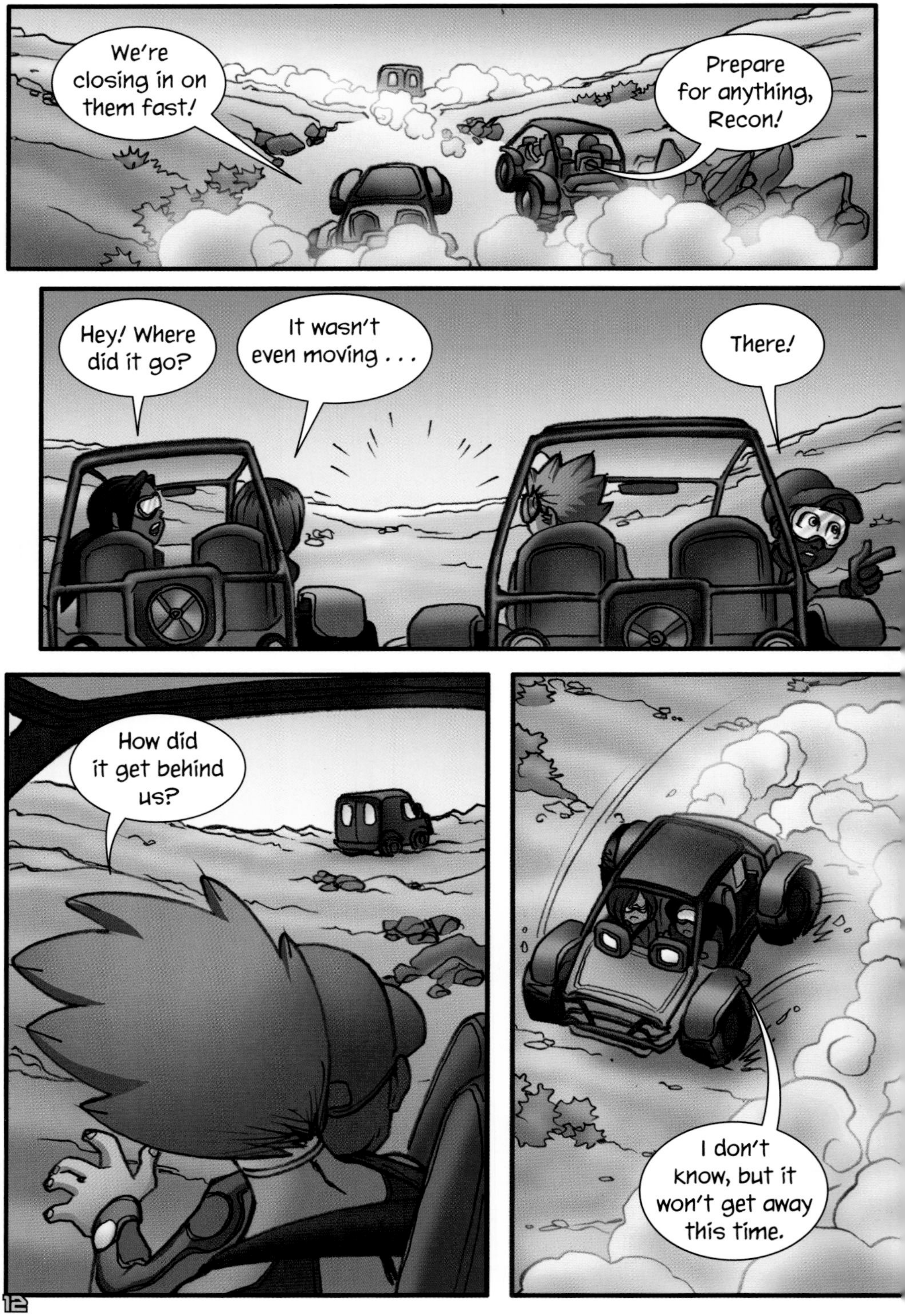
We're closing in on them fast!
Prepare for anything, Recon!
Hey! Where did it go?
It wasn't even moving . . .
There!
How did it get behind us?
I don't know, but it won't get away this time.

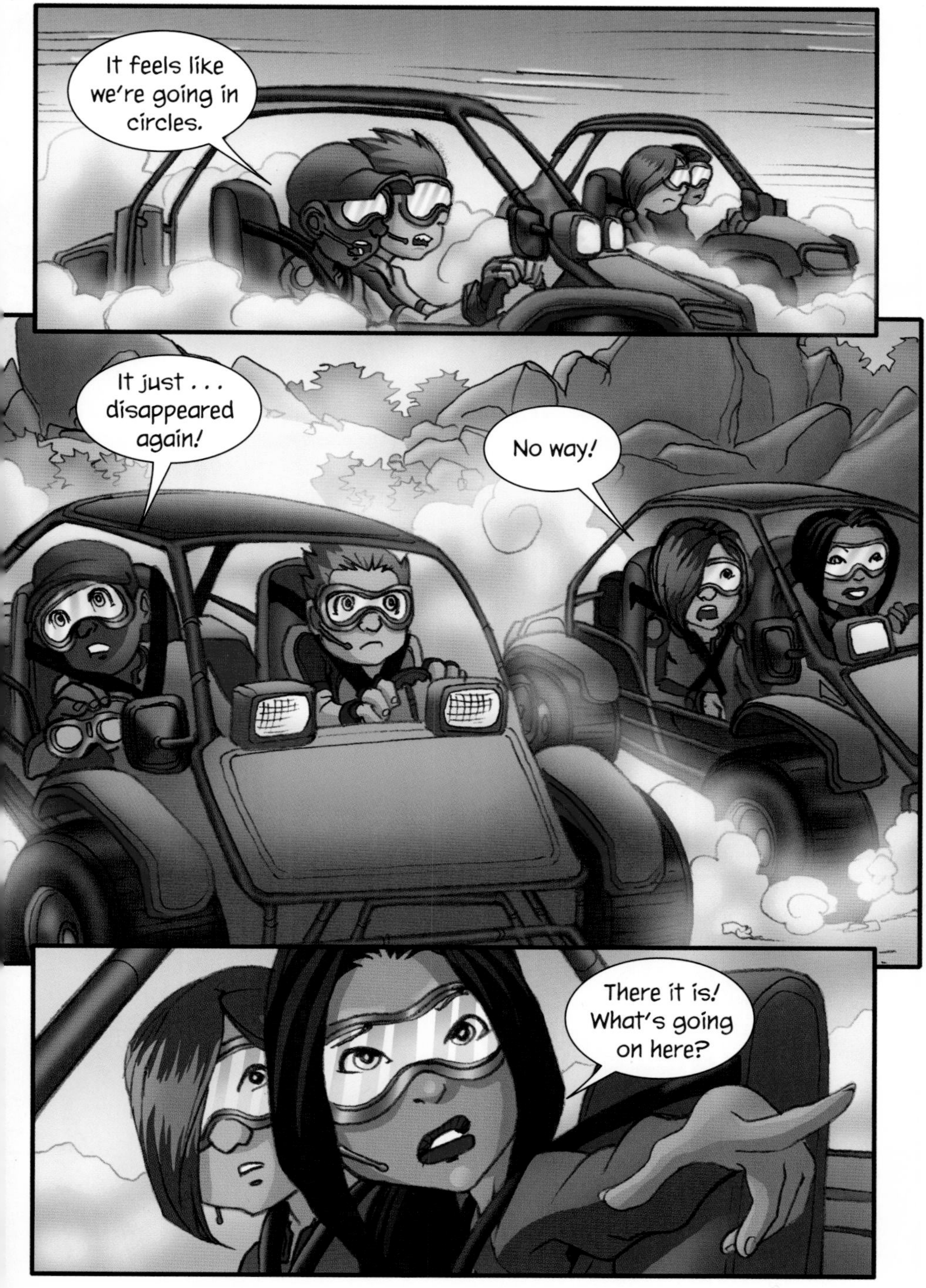
It feels like we're going in circles.
It just . . . disappeared again!
No way!
There it is! What's going on here?

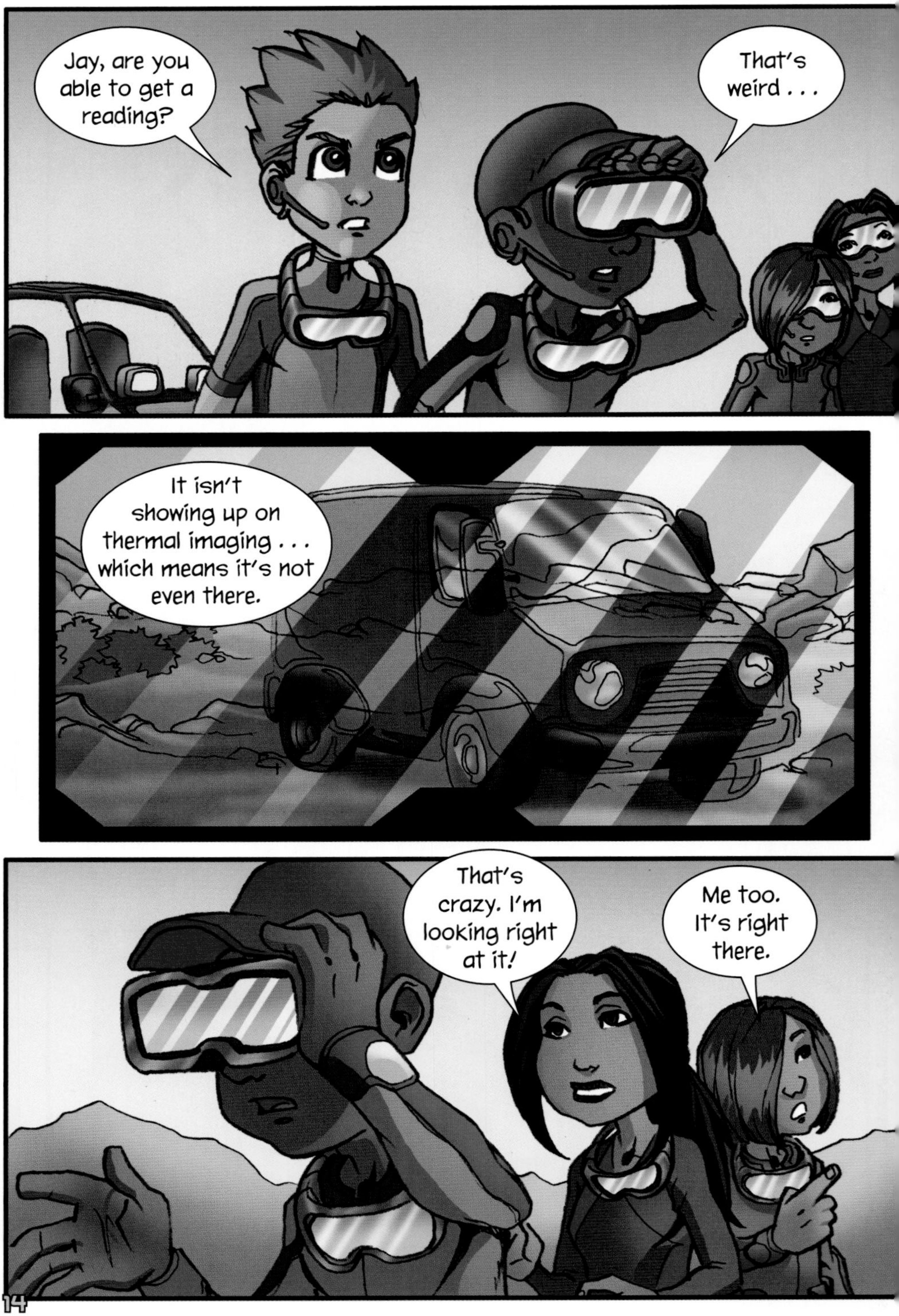

Jay, are you able to get a reading?
That's weird . . .
It isn't showing up on thermal imaging . . . which means it's not even there.
That's crazy. I'm looking right at it!
Me too. It's right there.

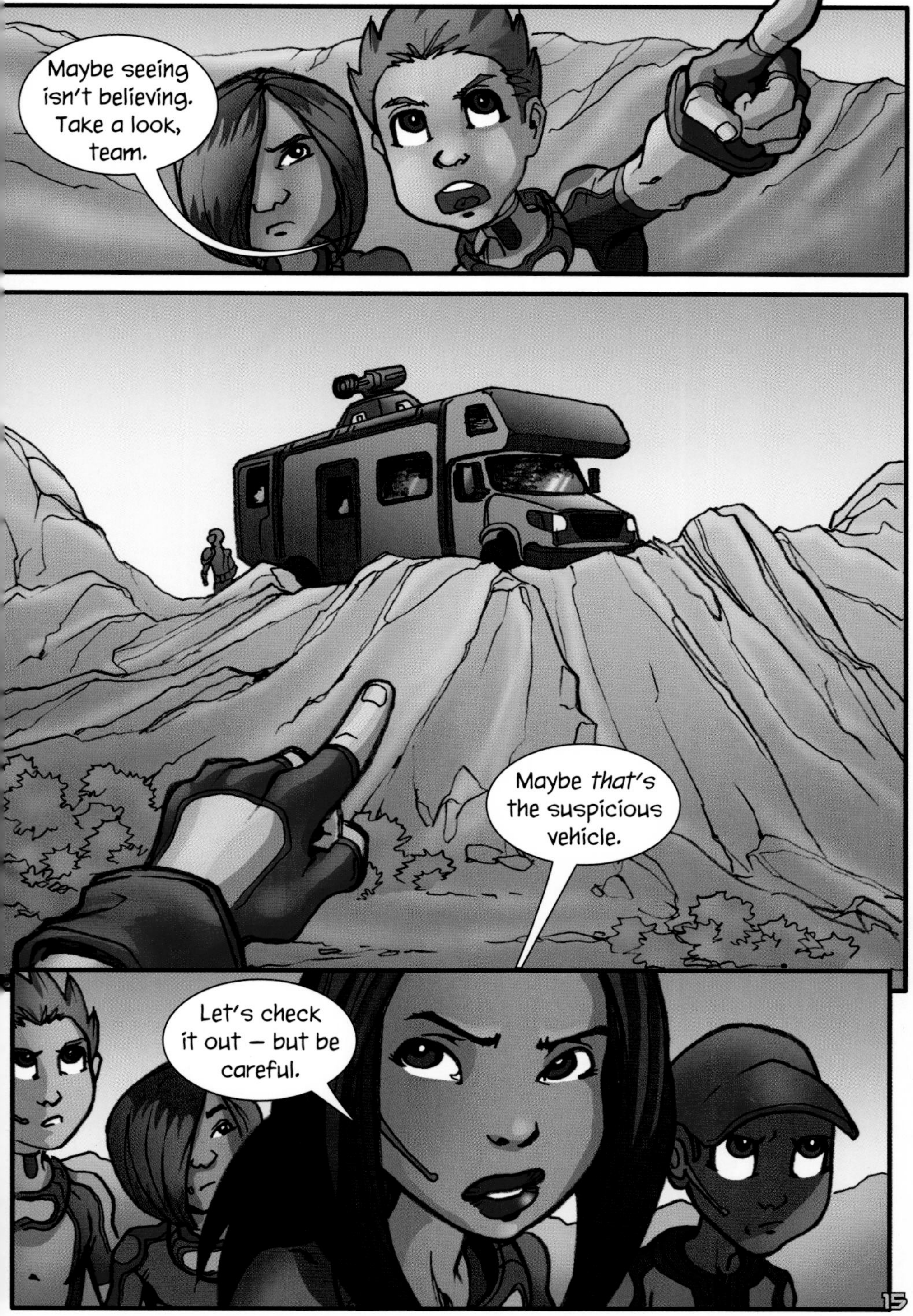
Maybe seeing isn't believing. Take a look, team.
Maybe *that's* the suspicious vehicle.
Let's check it out — but be careful.

SECTION

2

ACCESS GRANTED »»»

RYKER
COMPUTERS

128718
293829
9283
98289
89
1
109201
192091
1992

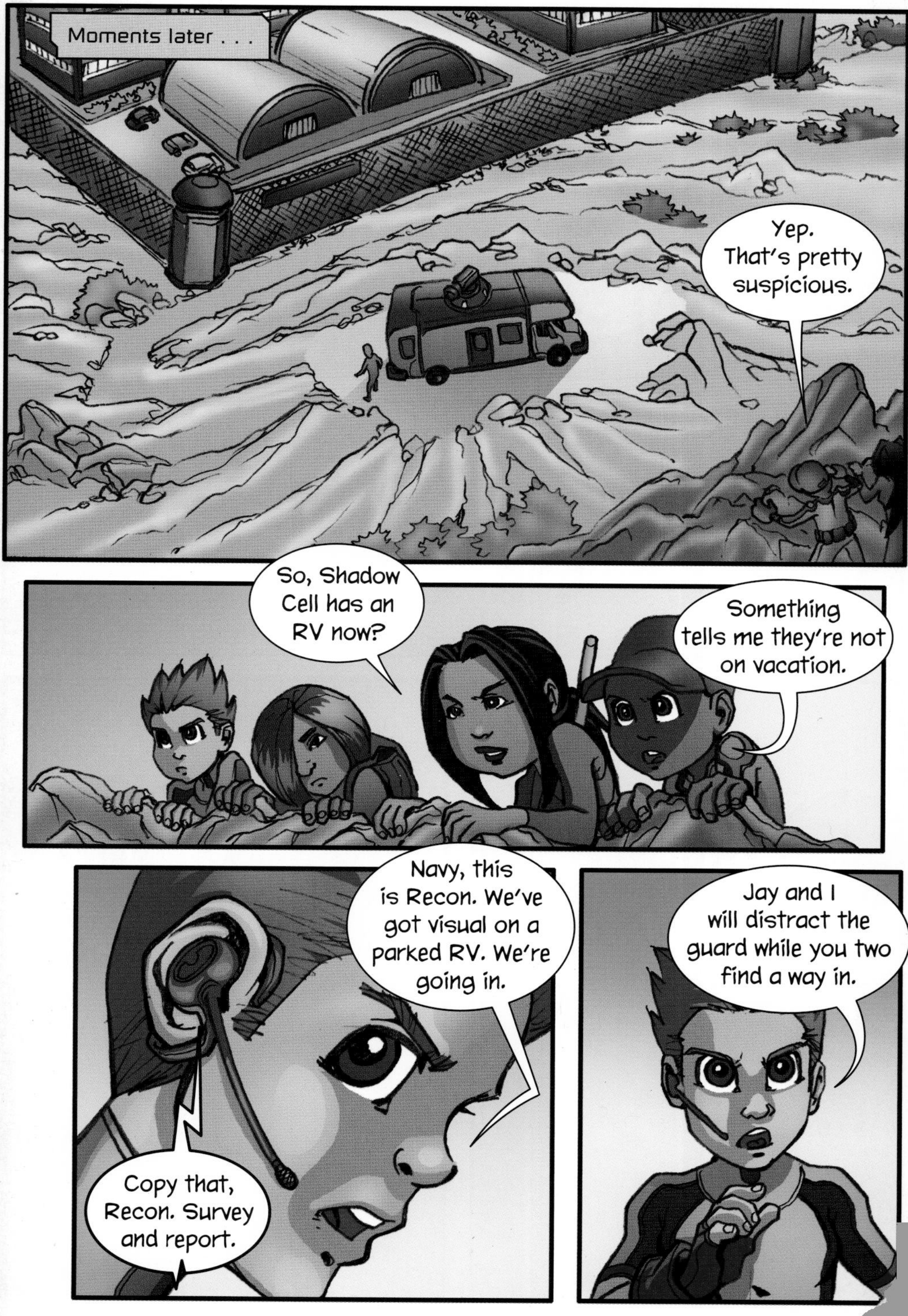
Moments later . . .
Yep. That's pretty suspicious.
So, Shadow Cell has an RV now?
Something tells me they're not on vacation.
Navy, this is Recon. We've got visual on a parked RV. We're going in.
Copy that, Recon. Survey and report.
Jay and I will distract the guard while you two find a way in.

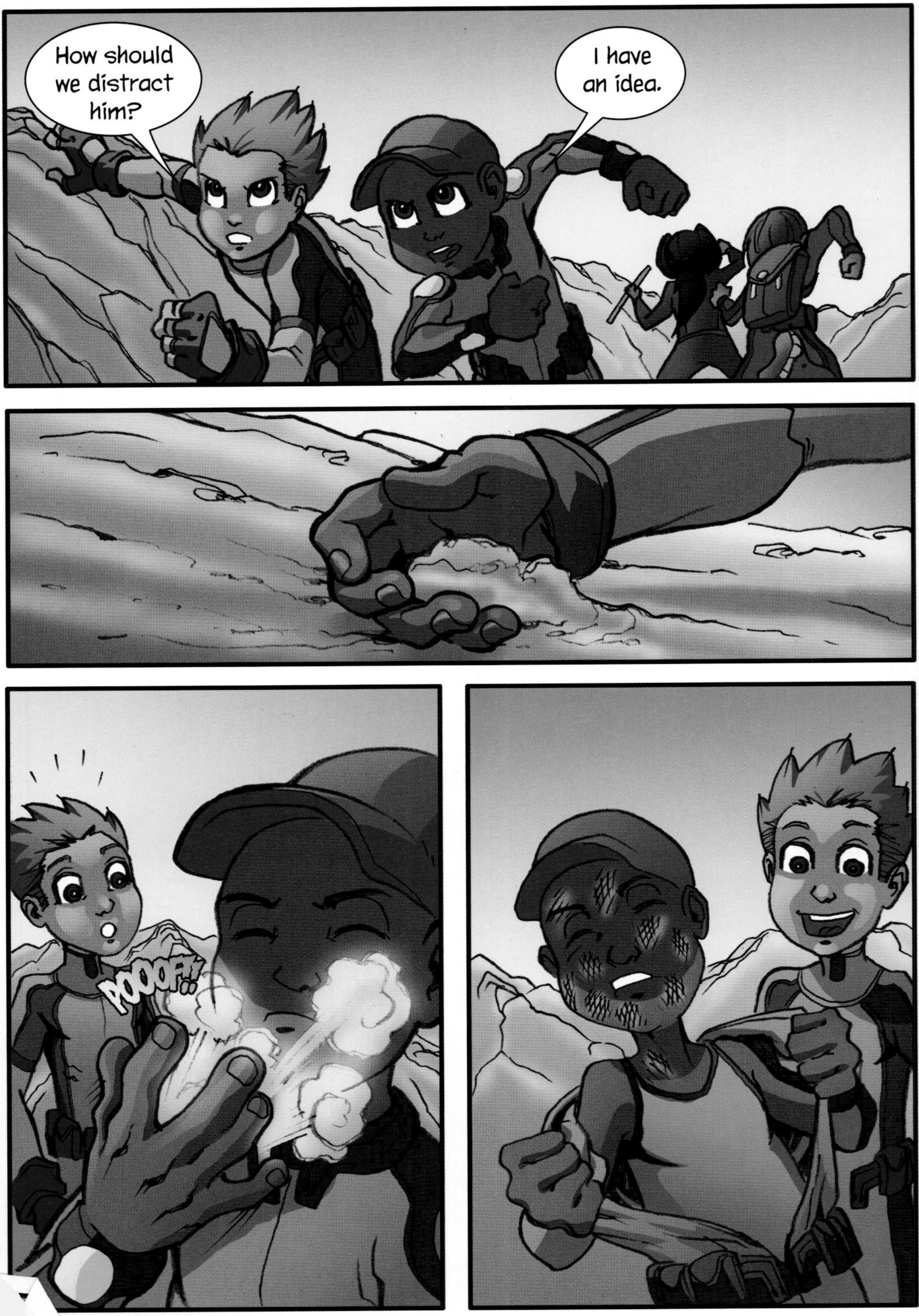

How should we distract him?
I have an idea.
POOOF!!

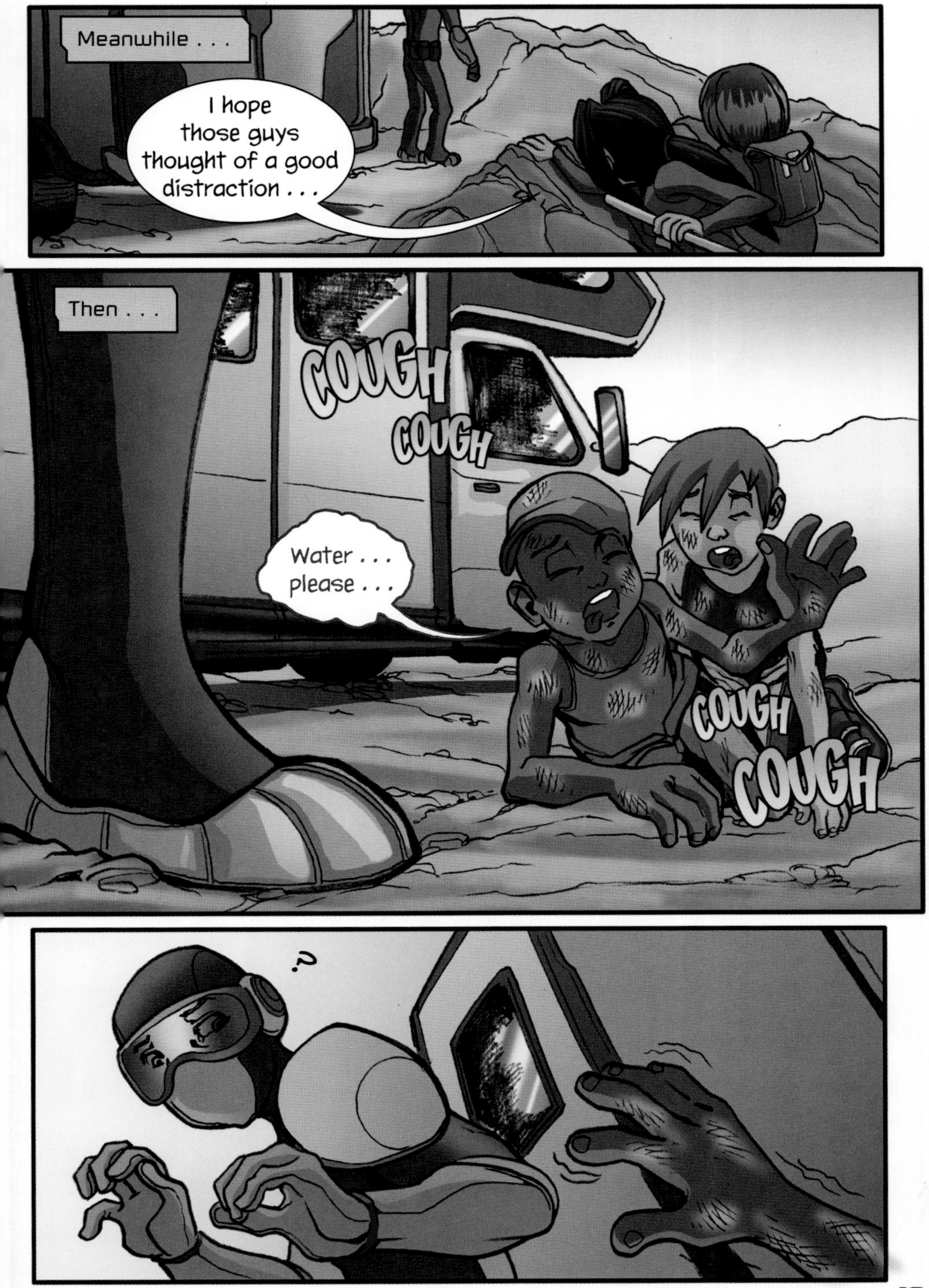

Meanwhile . . .
I hope those guys thought of a good distraction . . .
Then . . .
COUGH
COUGH
Water . . . please . . .
COUGH
COUGH
?

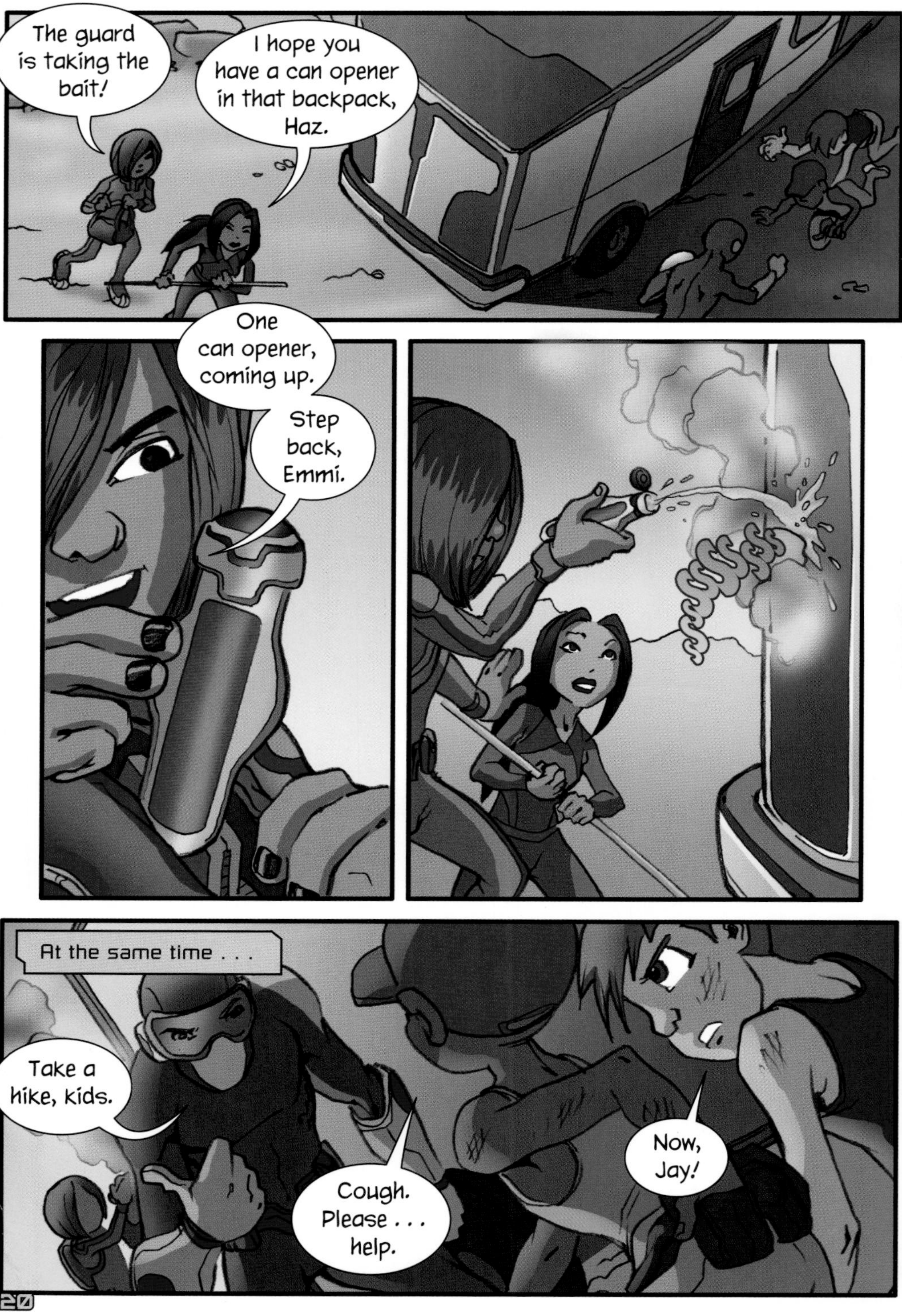

The guard is taking the bait!
I hope you have a can opener in that backpack, Haz.
One can opener, coming up.
Step back, Emmi.
At the same time . . .
Take a hike, kids.
Cough. Please . . . help.
Now, Jay!

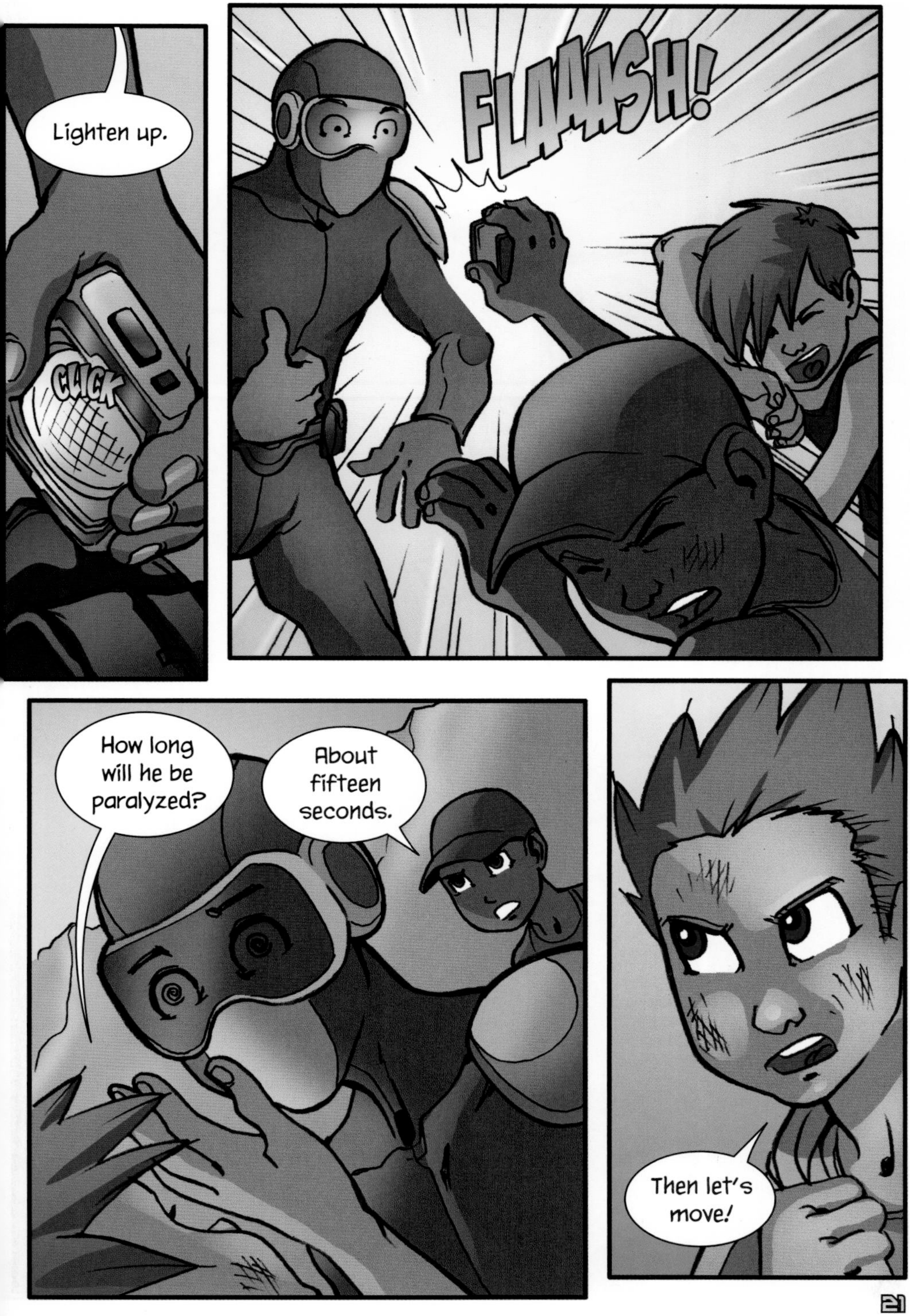
Lighten up.
CLICK
FLAAASH!
How long will he be paralyzed?
About fifteen seconds.
Then let's move!

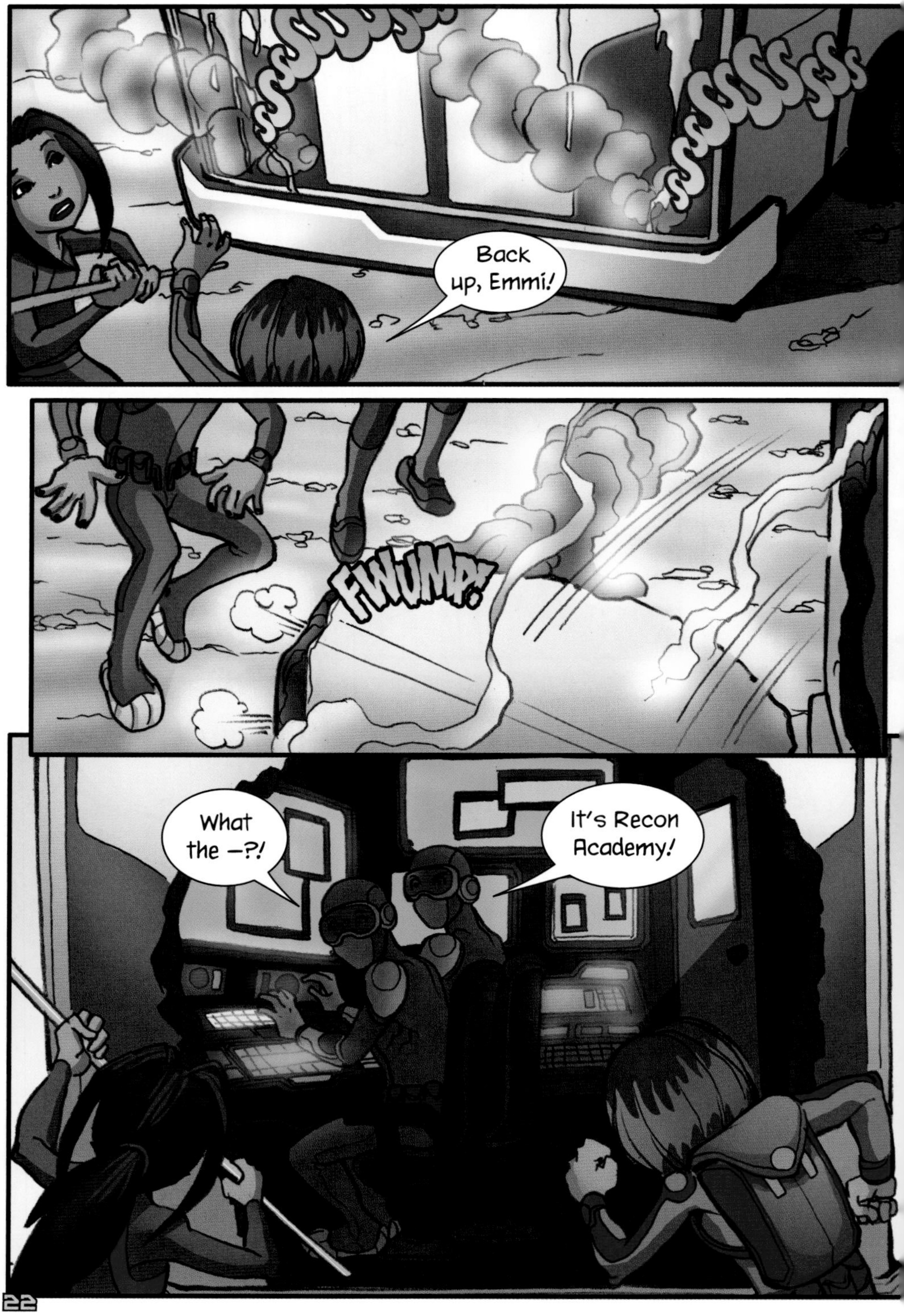
SSSSSSS
SSSSSSSSS
Back up, Emmi!
FWUMP!
What the —?!
It's Recon Academy!

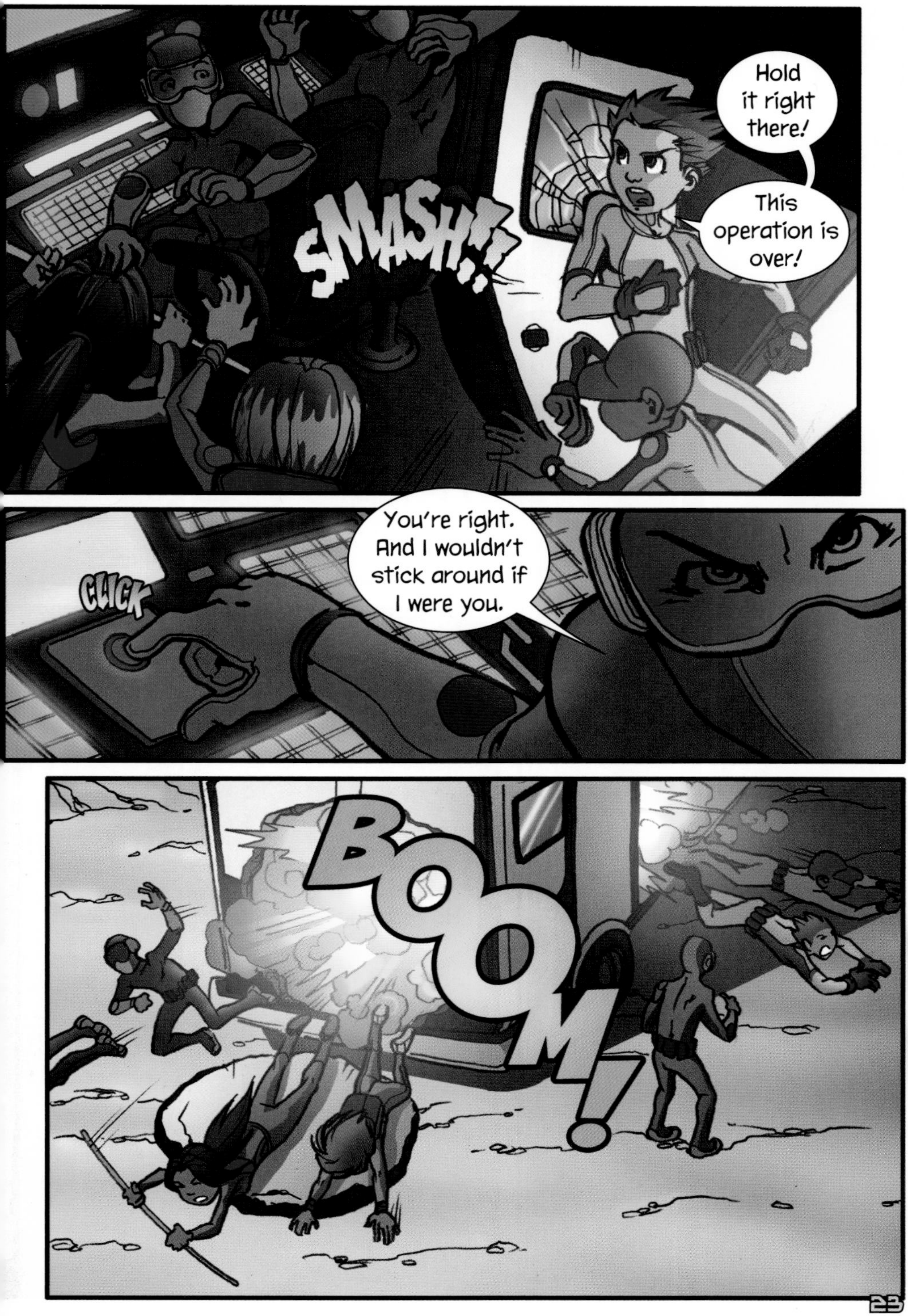
Hold it right there!
This operation is over!
SMASH!!!
CLICK
You're right. And I wouldn't stick around if I were you.
BOOM!

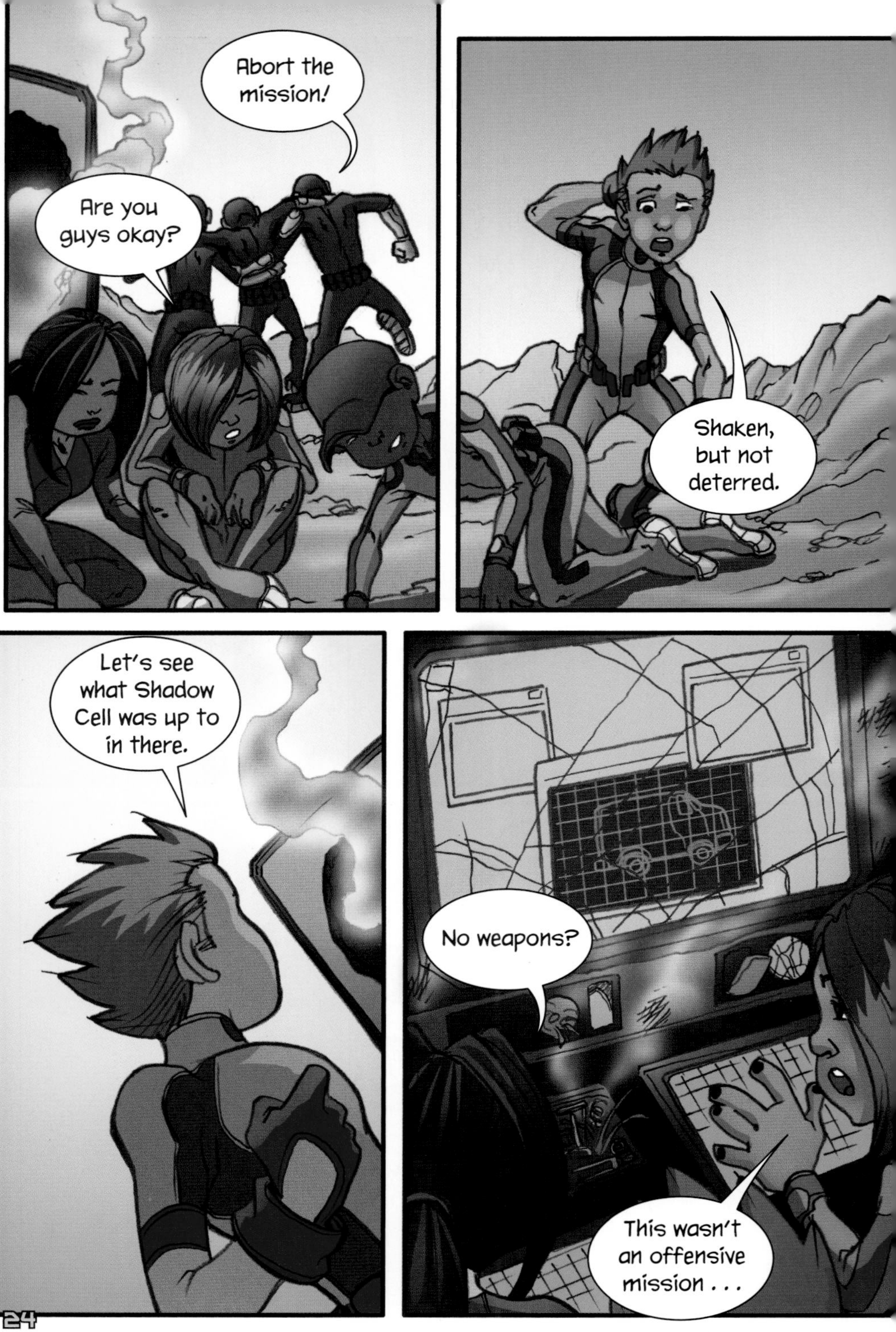
Abort the mission!
Are you guys okay?
Shaken, but not deterred.
Let's see what Shadow Cell was up to in there.
No weapons?
This wasn't an offensive mission . . .

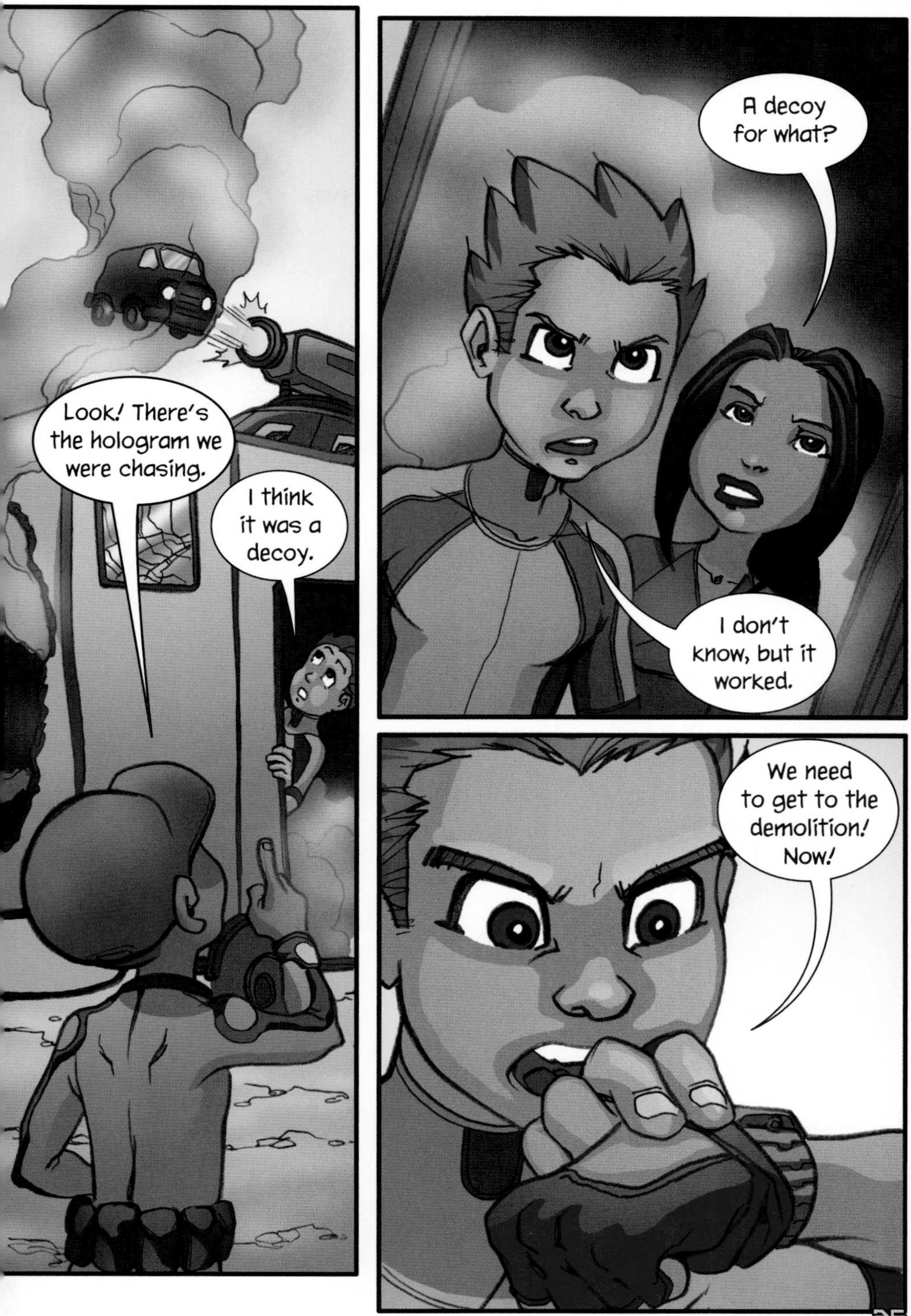
Look! There's the hologram we were chasing.
I think it was a decoy.
A decoy for what?
I don't know, but it worked.
We need to get to the demolition! Now!

SECTION 3

ACCESS GRANTED))))

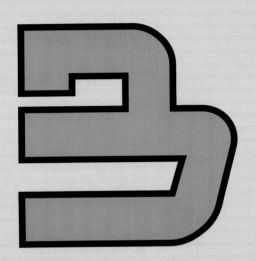

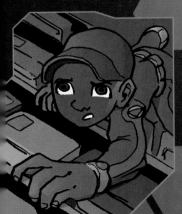

JAY
GADGETRY

128718
293829
9283
98289
89
1
109201
192091
1992

1827178 198291821 918298

1827178 198291821 918298

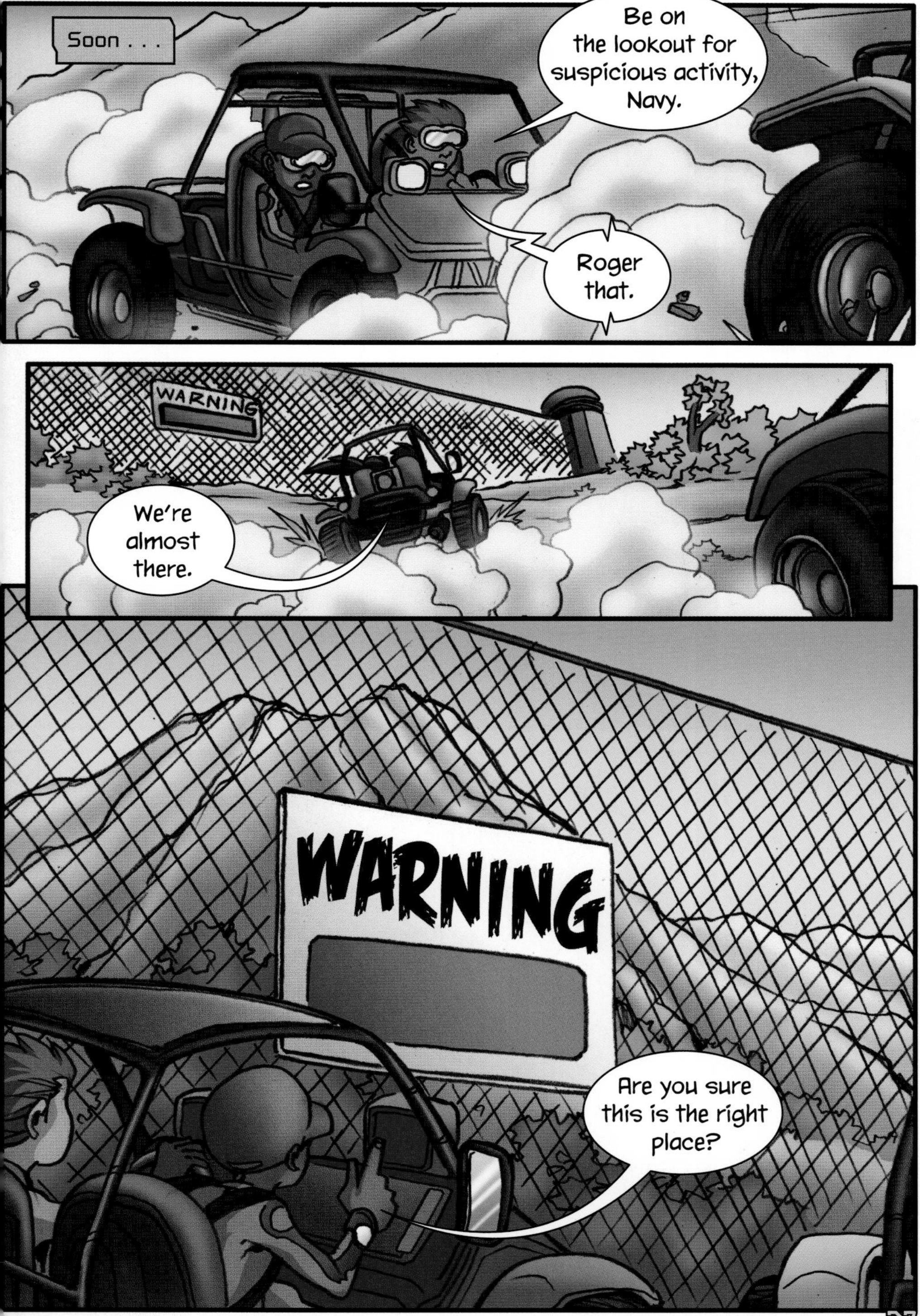
Soon . . .
Be on the lookout for suspicious activity, Navy.
Roger that.
WARNING
We're almost there.
WARNING
Are you sure this is the right place?

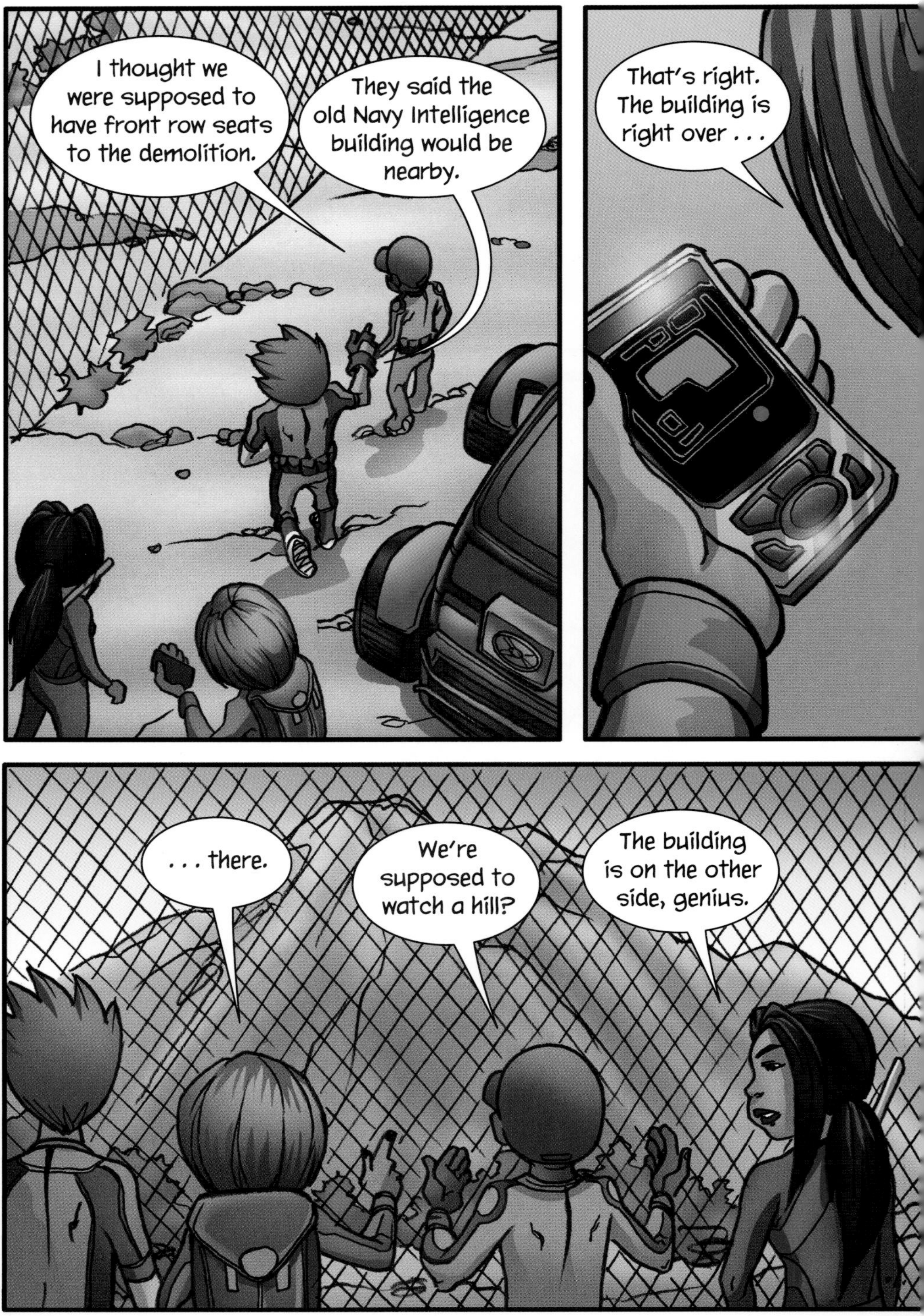

I thought we were supposed to have front row seats to the demolition.
They said the old Navy Intelligence building would be nearby.
That's right. The building is right over . . .
. . . there.
We're supposed to watch a hill?
The building is on the other side, genius.

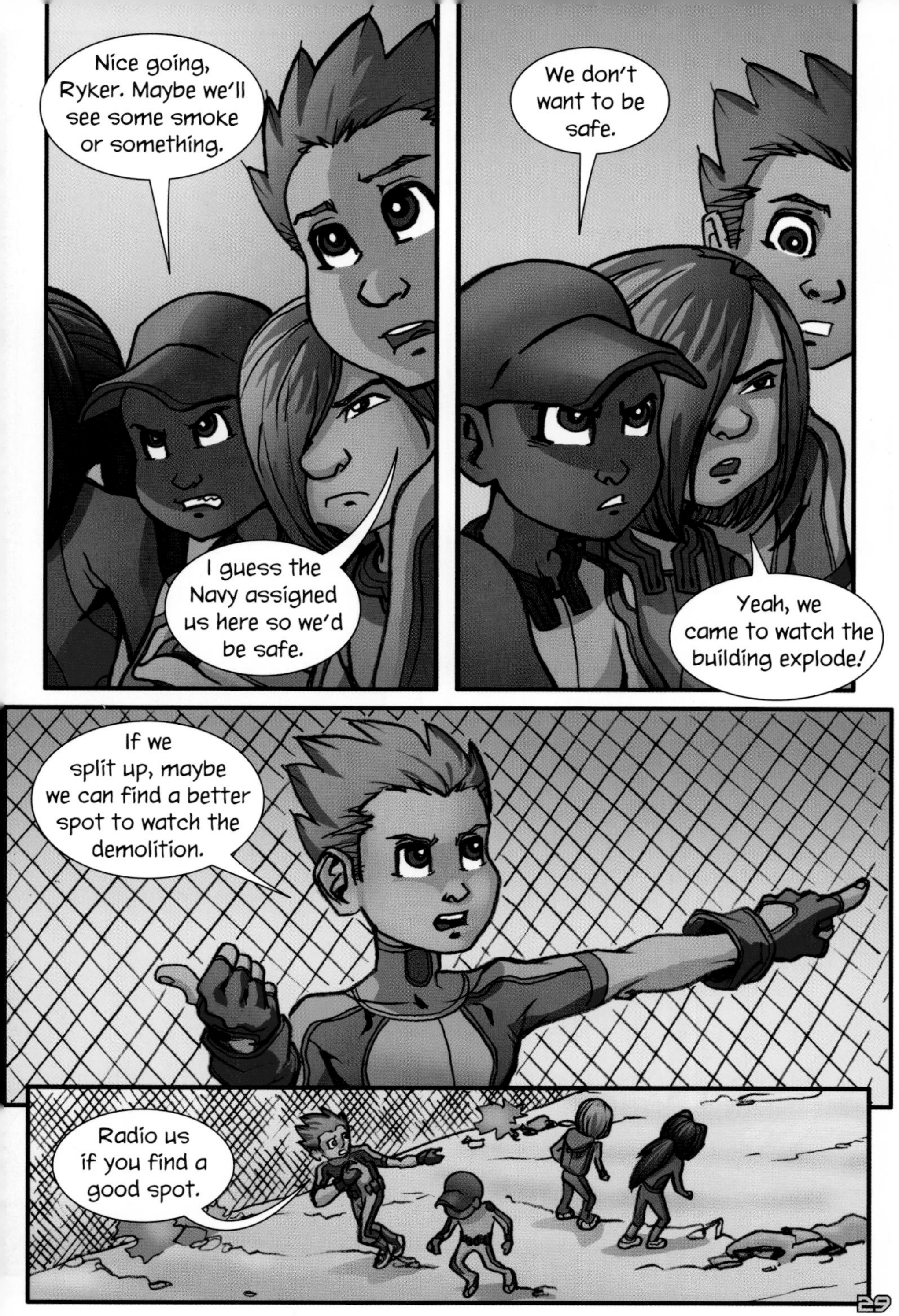
Nice going, Ryker. Maybe we'll see some smoke or something.
I guess the Navy assigned us here so we'd be safe.
We don't want to be safe.
Yeah, we came to watch the building explode!
If we split up, maybe we can find a better spot to watch the demolition.
Radio us if you find a good spot.

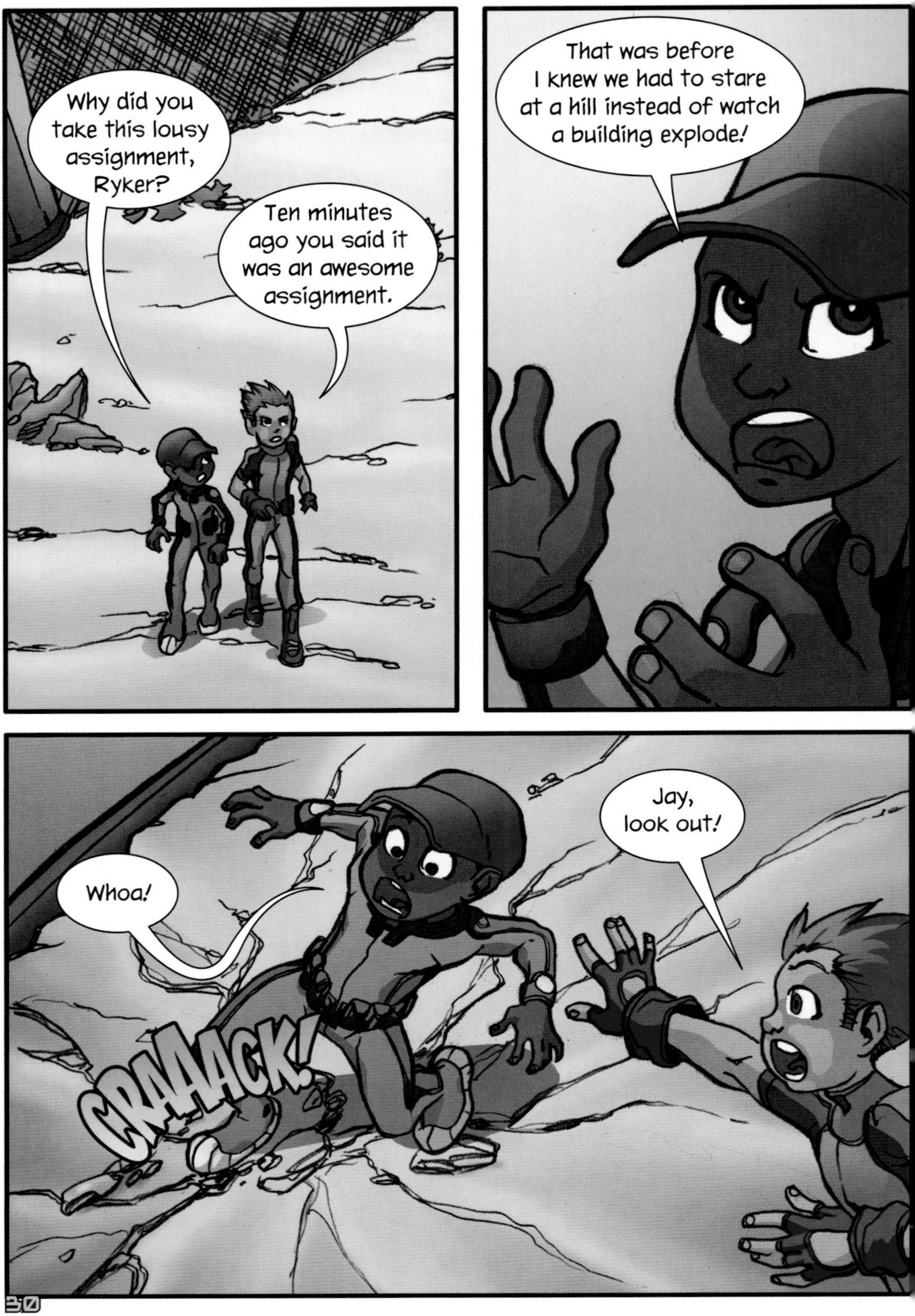
Why did you take this lousy assignment, Ryker?
Ten minutes ago you said it was an awesome assignment.
That was before I knew we had to stare at a hill instead of watch a building explode!
CRAAACK!
Whoa!
Jay, look out!

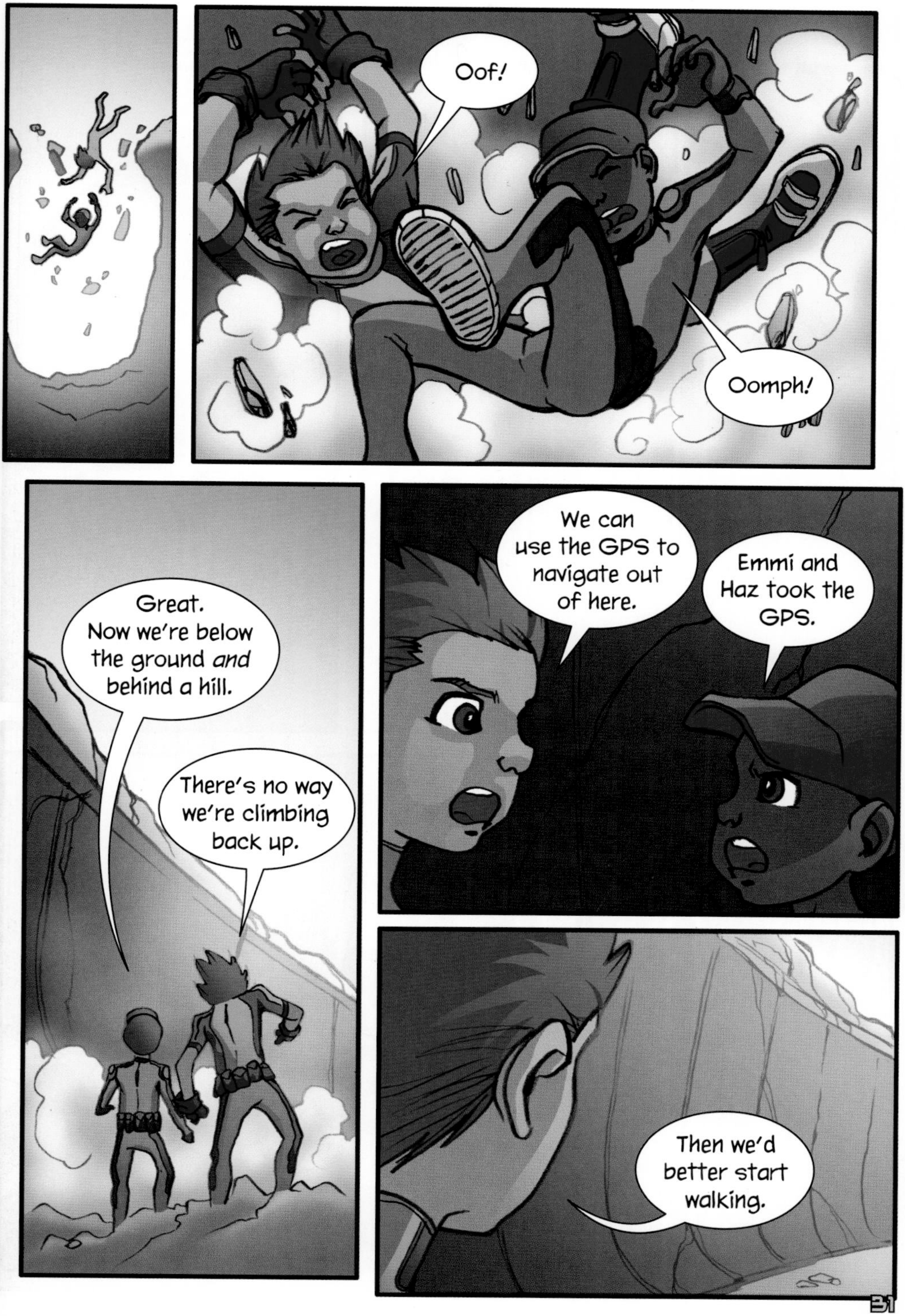
Oof!
Oomph!
Great. Now we're below the ground *and* behind a hill.
There's no way we're climbing back up.
We can use the GPS to navigate out of here.
Emmi and Haz took the GPS.
Then we'd better start walking.

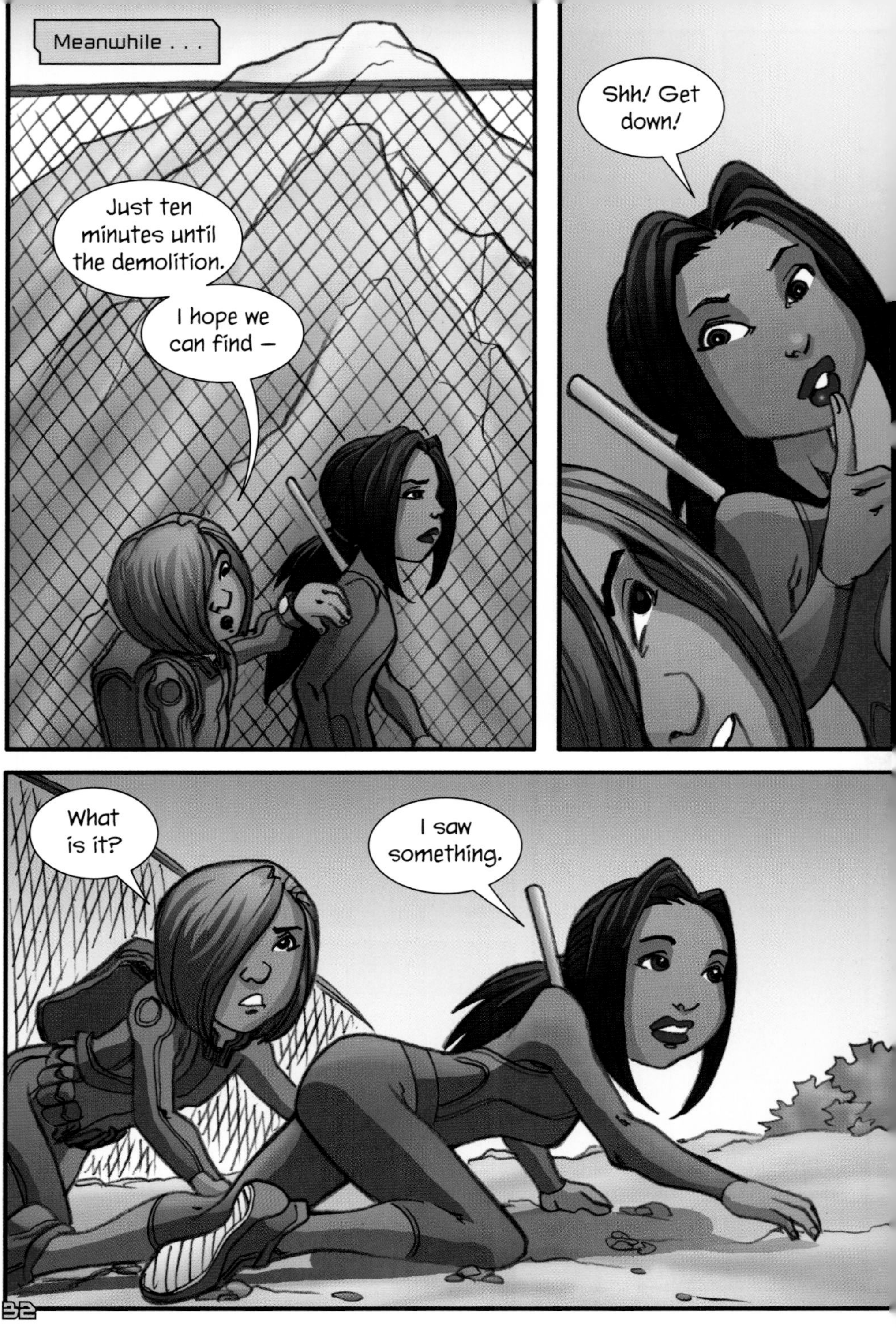

Meanwhile . . .
Just ten minutes until the demolition.
I hope we can find —
Shh! Get down!
What is it?
I saw something.

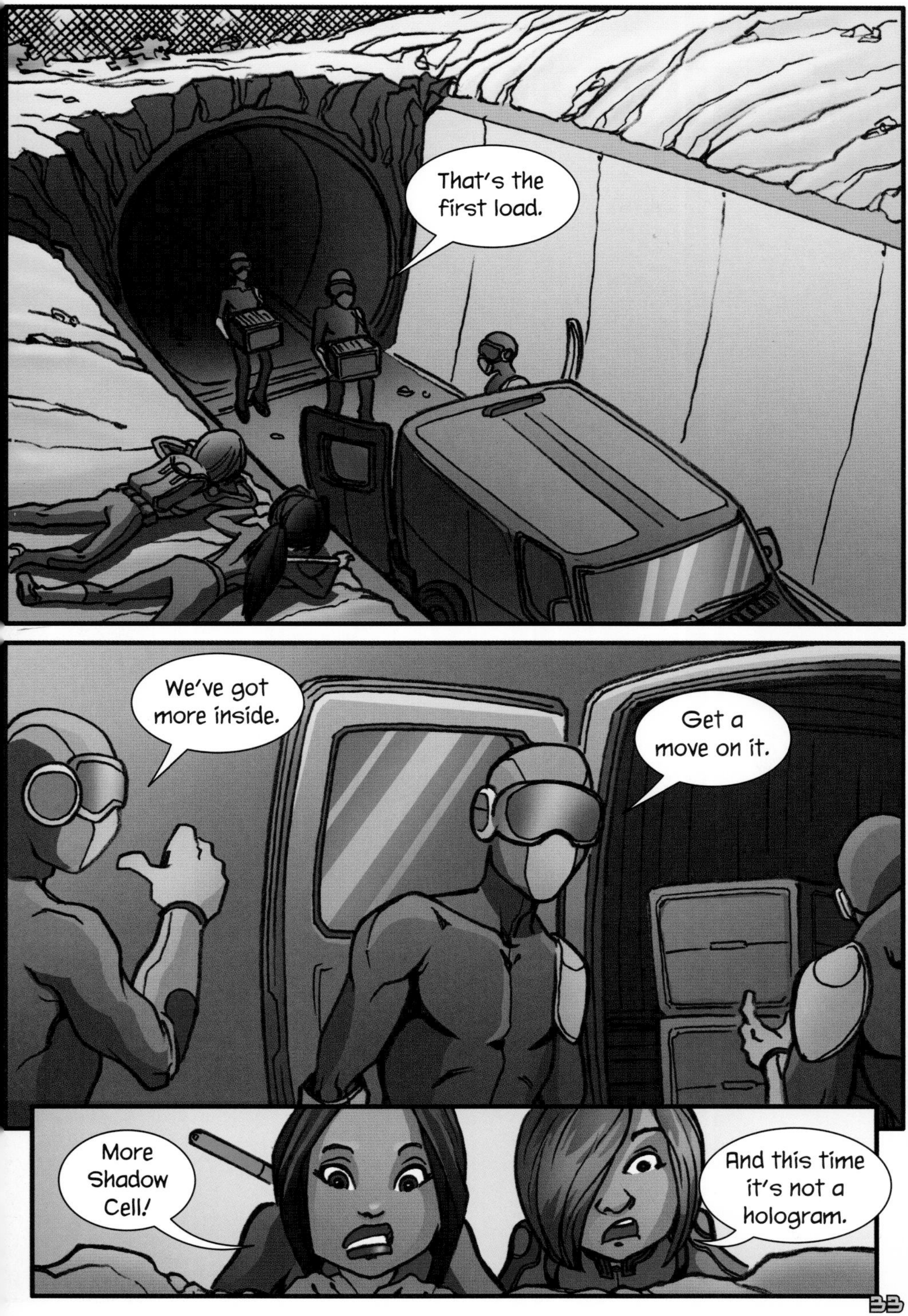
That's the first load.
We've got more inside.
Get a move on it.
More Shadow Cell!
And this time it's not a hologram.

SECTION

4

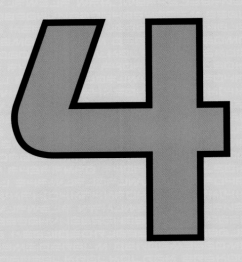

ACCESS GRANTED 〉〉〉〉

HAZMAT
FORENSICS

8579
1564574
109201
192091
1992
745979

128718
293829
9286
98289
88
1
109201
192091
1992

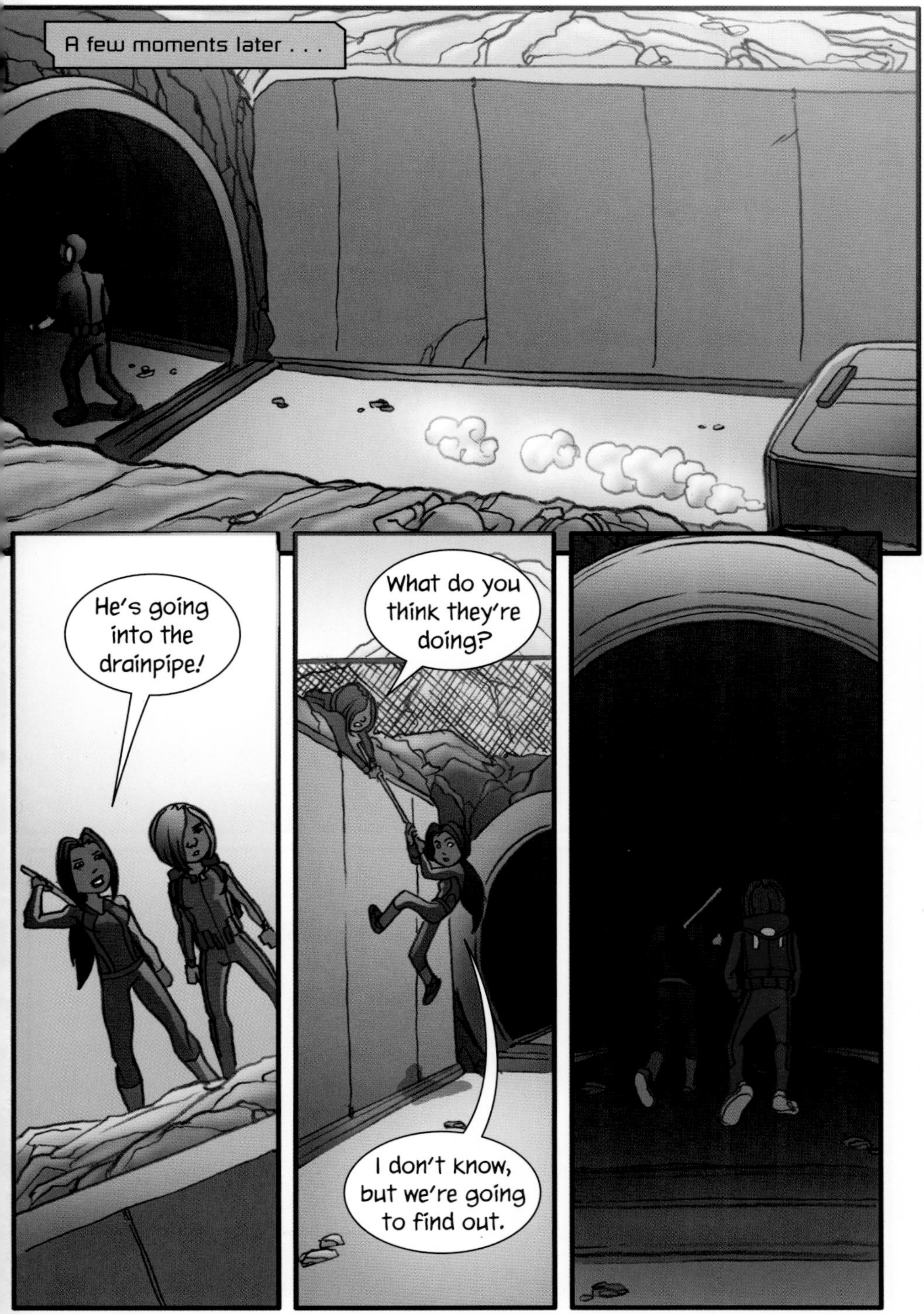

A few moments later . . .
He's going into the drainpipe!
What do you think they're doing?
I don't know, but we're going to find out.

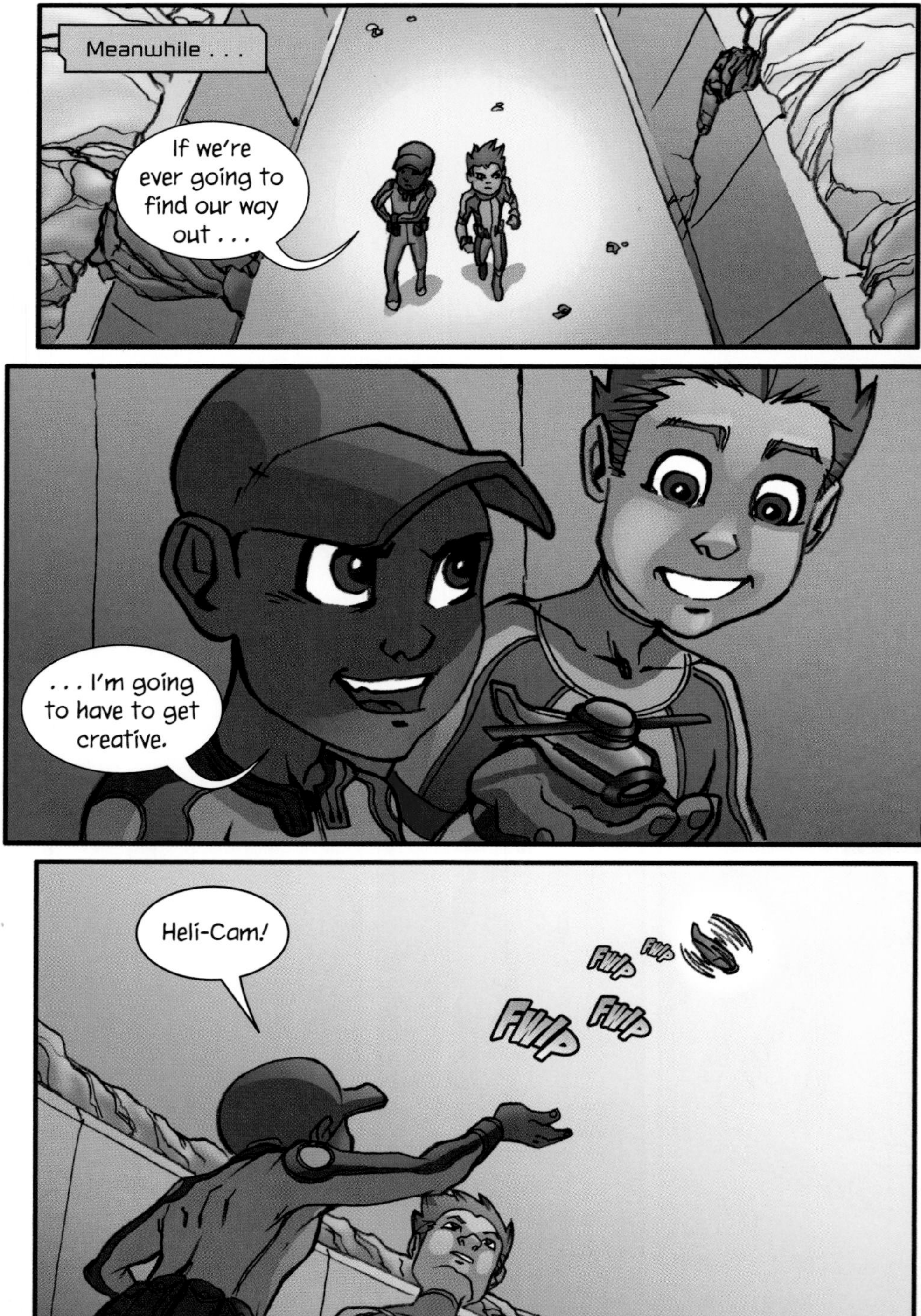
Meanwhile . . .
If we're ever going to find our way out . . .
. . . I'm going to have to get creative.
Heli-Cam!
FWIP
FWIP
FWIP
FWIP

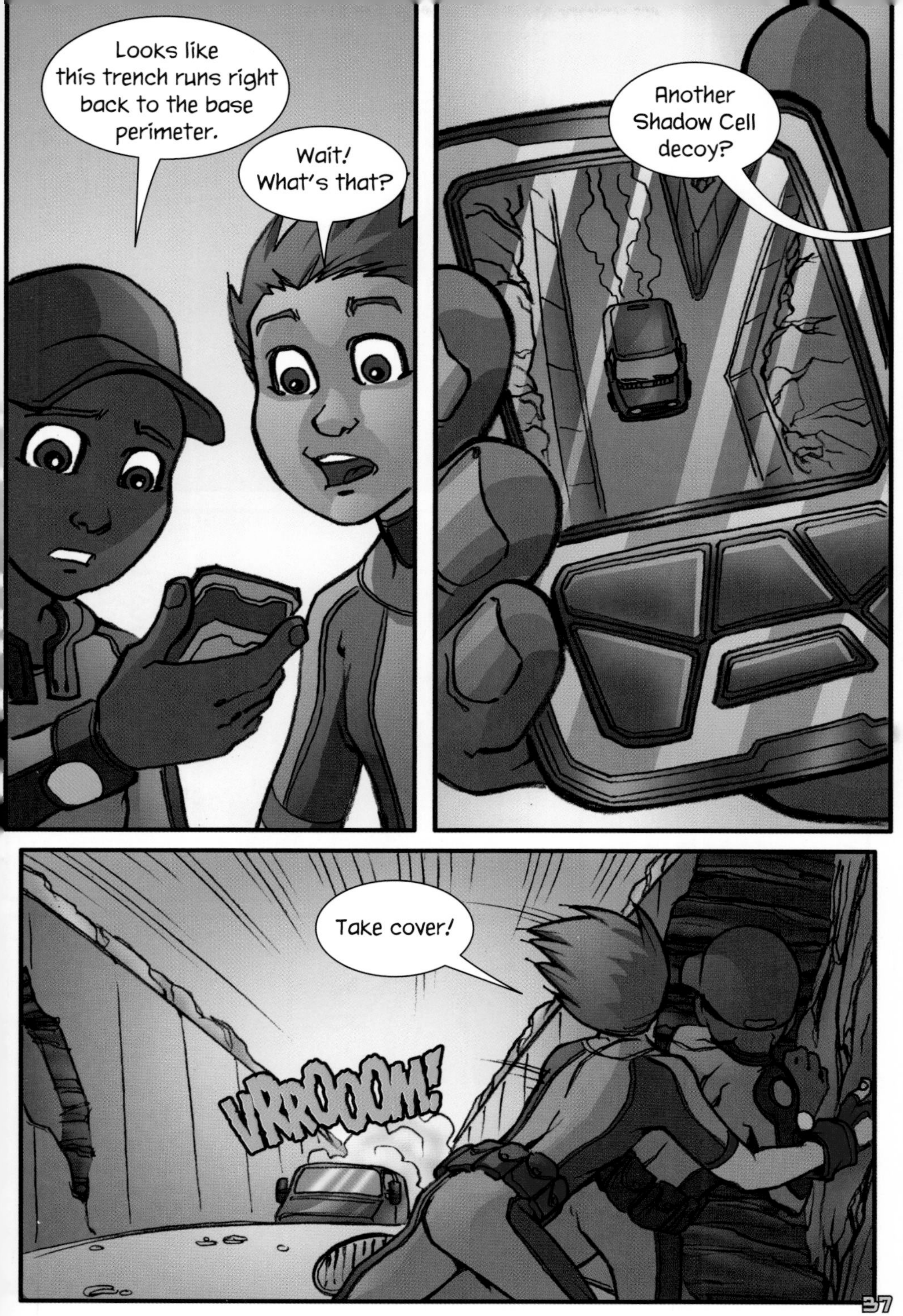
Looks like this trench runs right back to the base perimeter.
Wait! What's that?
Another Shadow Cell decoy?
Take cover!
VRROOOM!

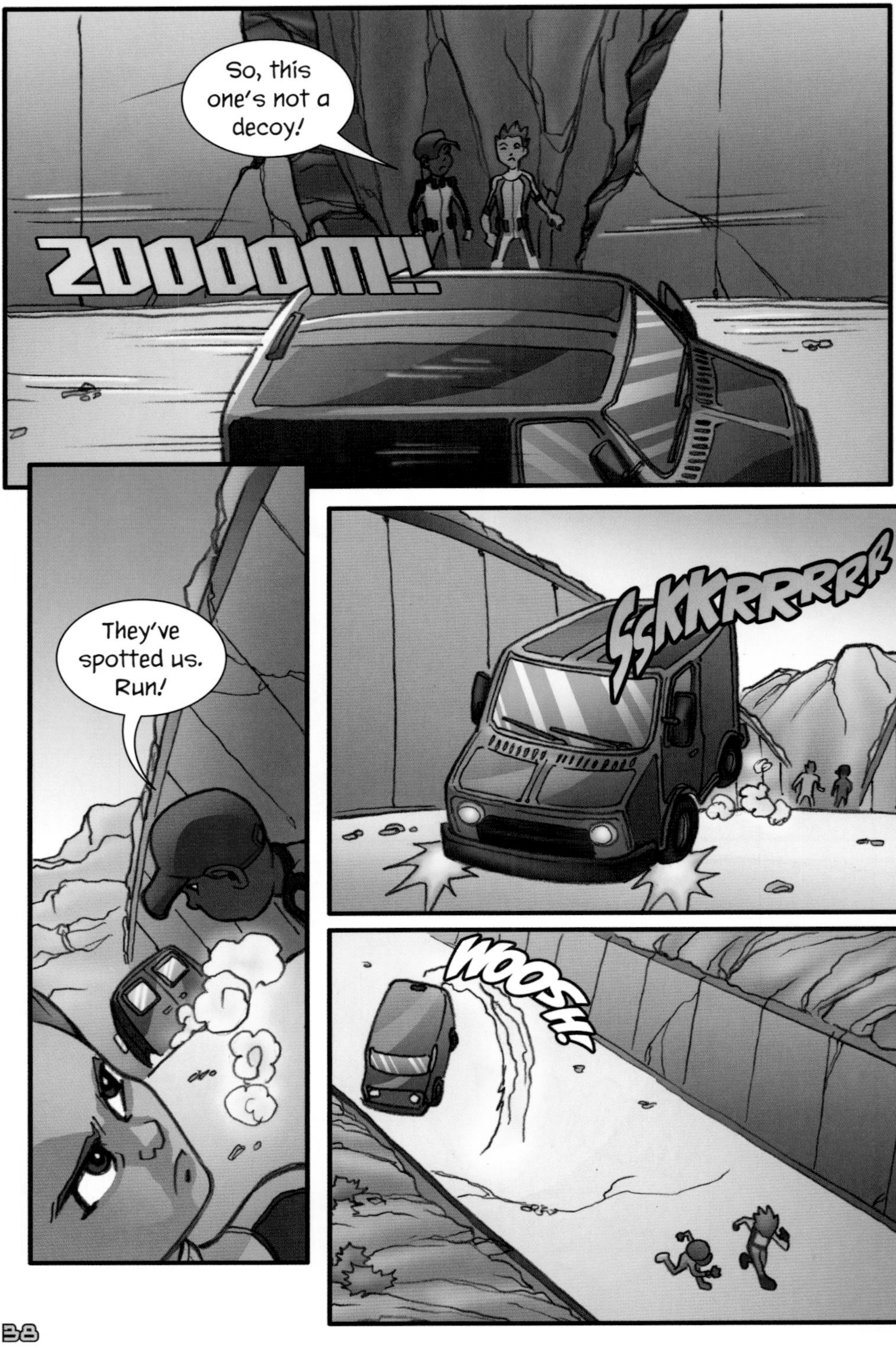
So, this one's not a decoy!
ZOOOOM!!
They've spotted us. Run!
SSKKRRRRRR
WOOSH!

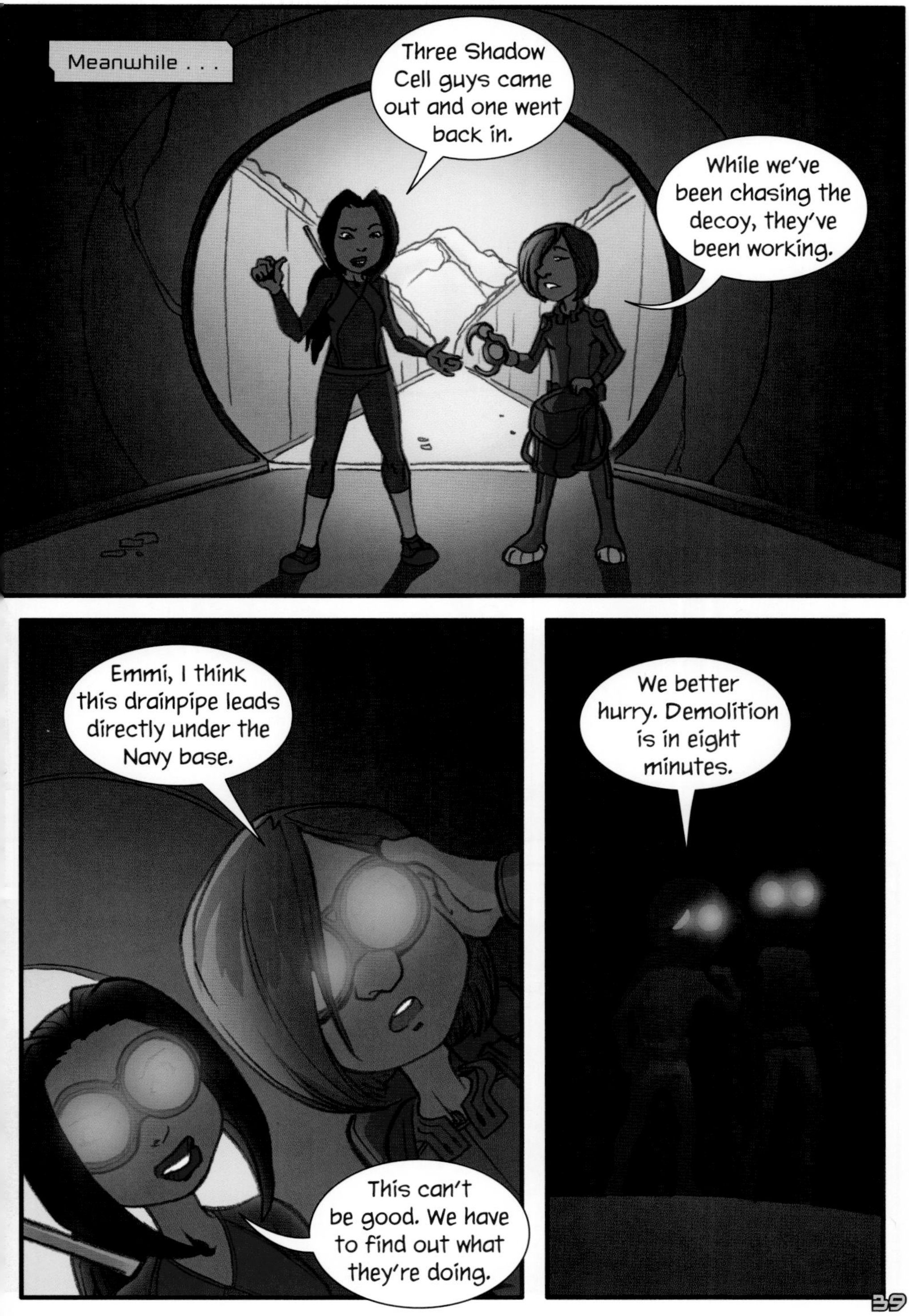
Meanwhile . . .
Three Shadow Cell guys came out and one went back in.
While we've been chasing the decoy, they've been working.
Emmi, I think this drainpipe leads directly under the Navy base.
This can't be good. We have to find out what they're doing.
We better hurry. Demolition is in eight minutes.

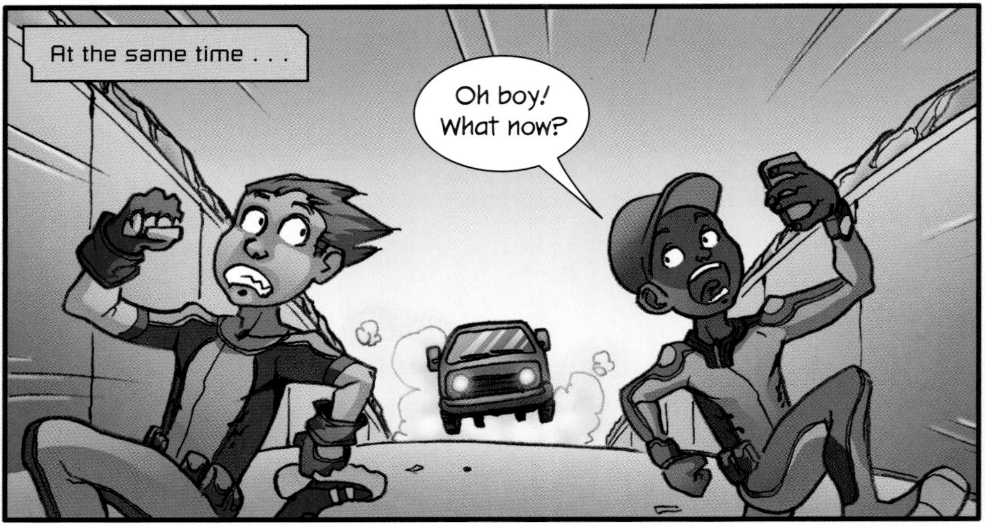
At the same time . . .
Oh boy! What now?

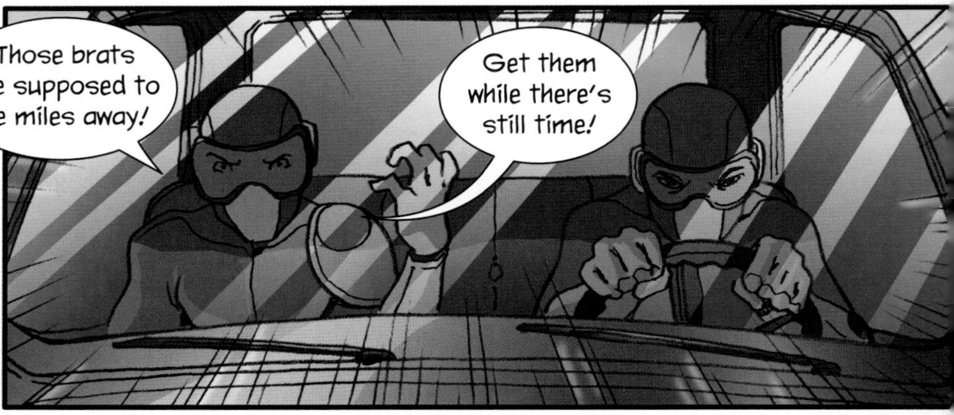
Those brats are supposed to be miles away!
Get them while there's still time!

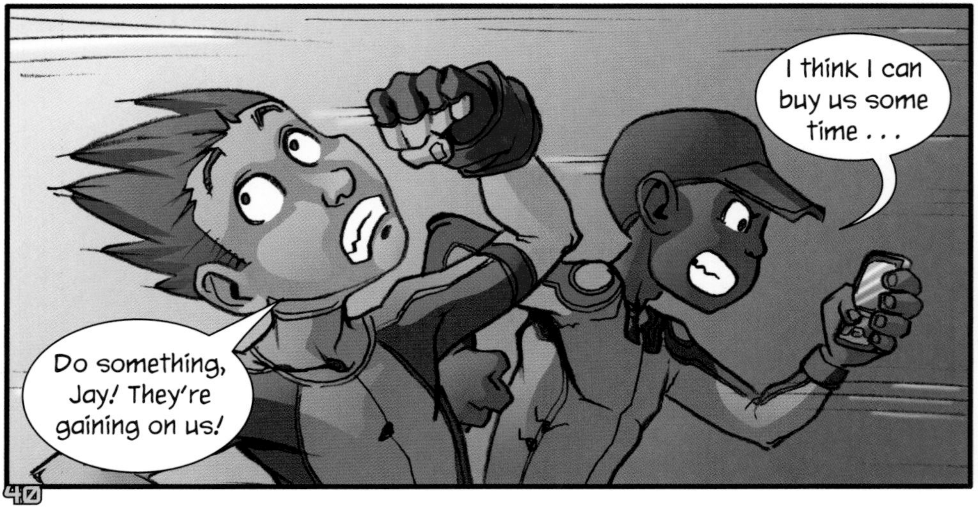
I think I can buy us some time . . .
Do something, Jay! They're gaining on us!

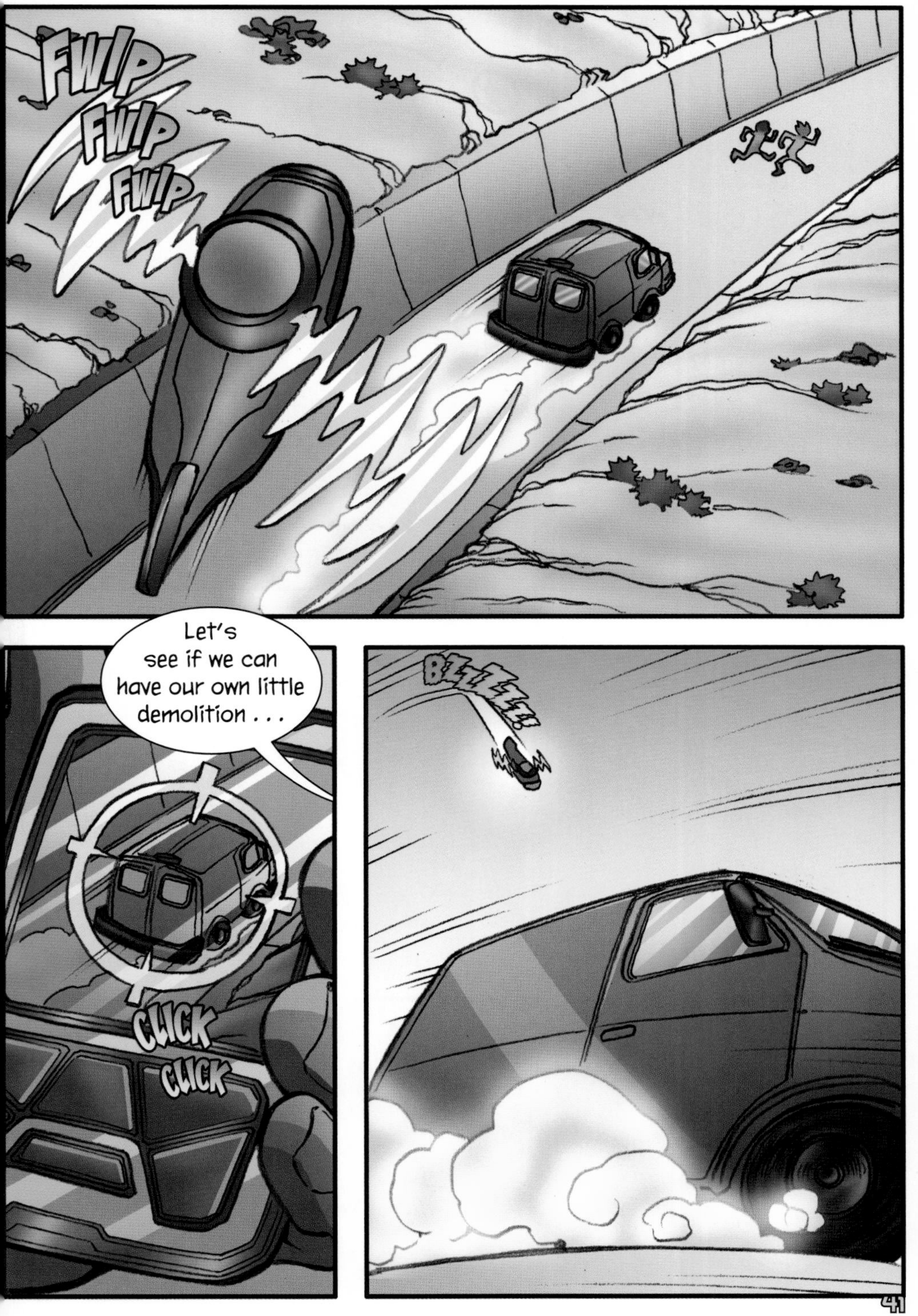
FWIP
FWIP
FWIP
Let's see if we can have our own little demolition . . .
CLICK
CLICK

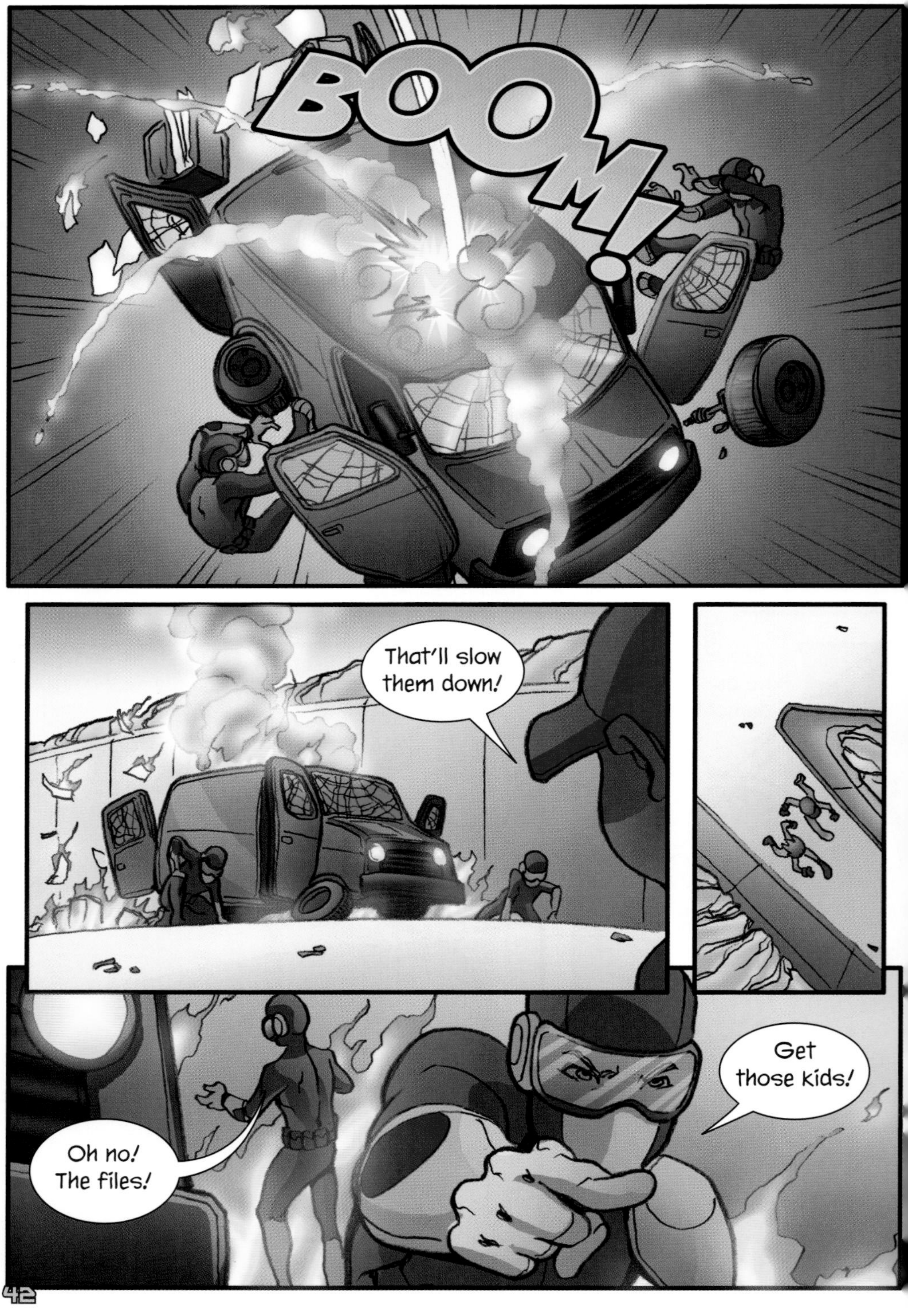
BOOM!
That'll slow them down!
Get those kids!
Oh no! The files!

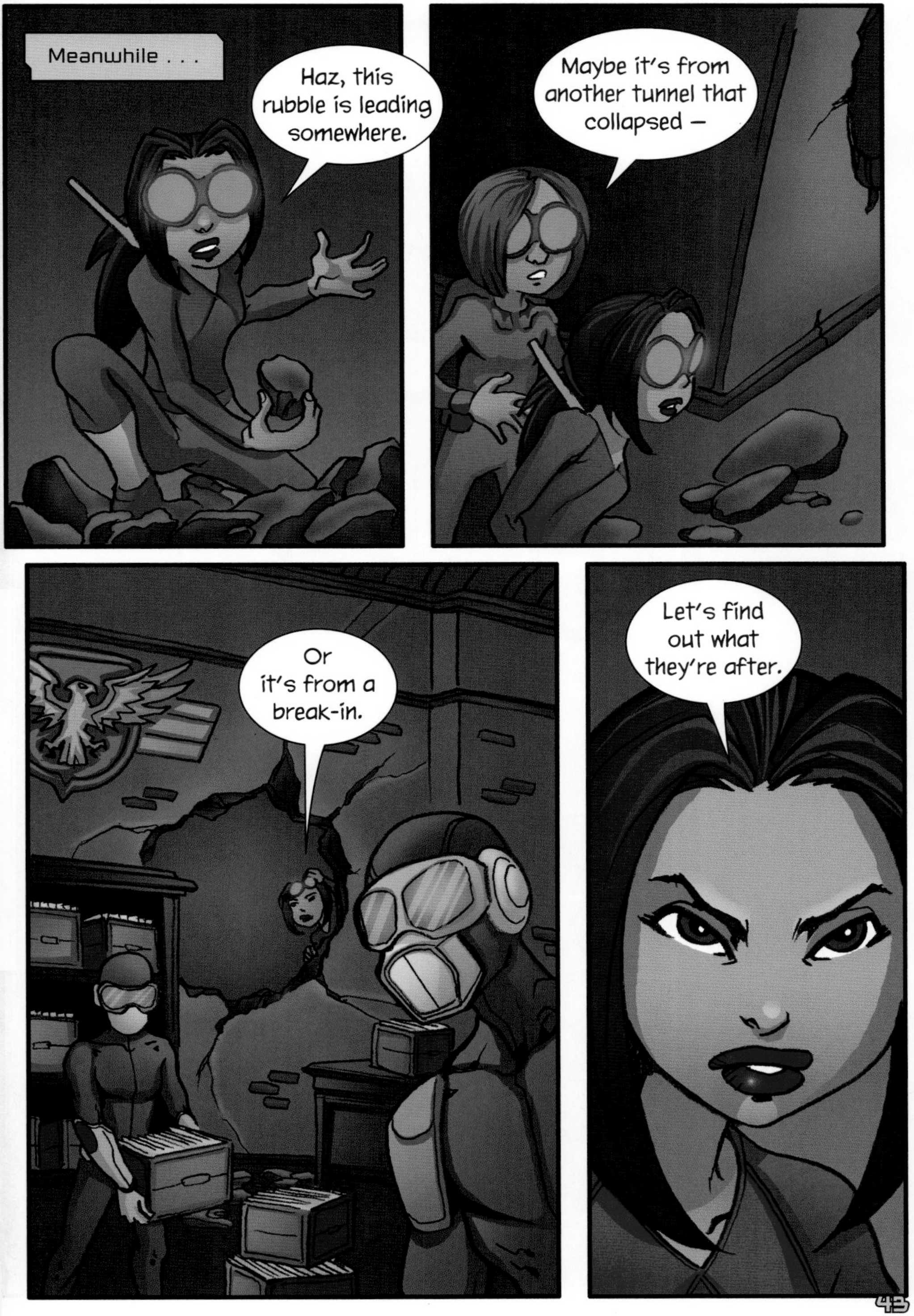
Meanwhile . . .
Haz, this rubble is leading somewhere.
Maybe it's from another tunnel that collapsed –
Or it's from a break-in.
Let's find out what they're after.

SECTION

5

ACCESS GRANTED >>>>

EMMI
MARTIAL ARTS

128718
293829
9283
98289
89
1
109201
192091
1992

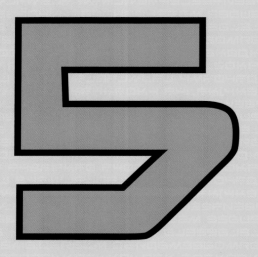

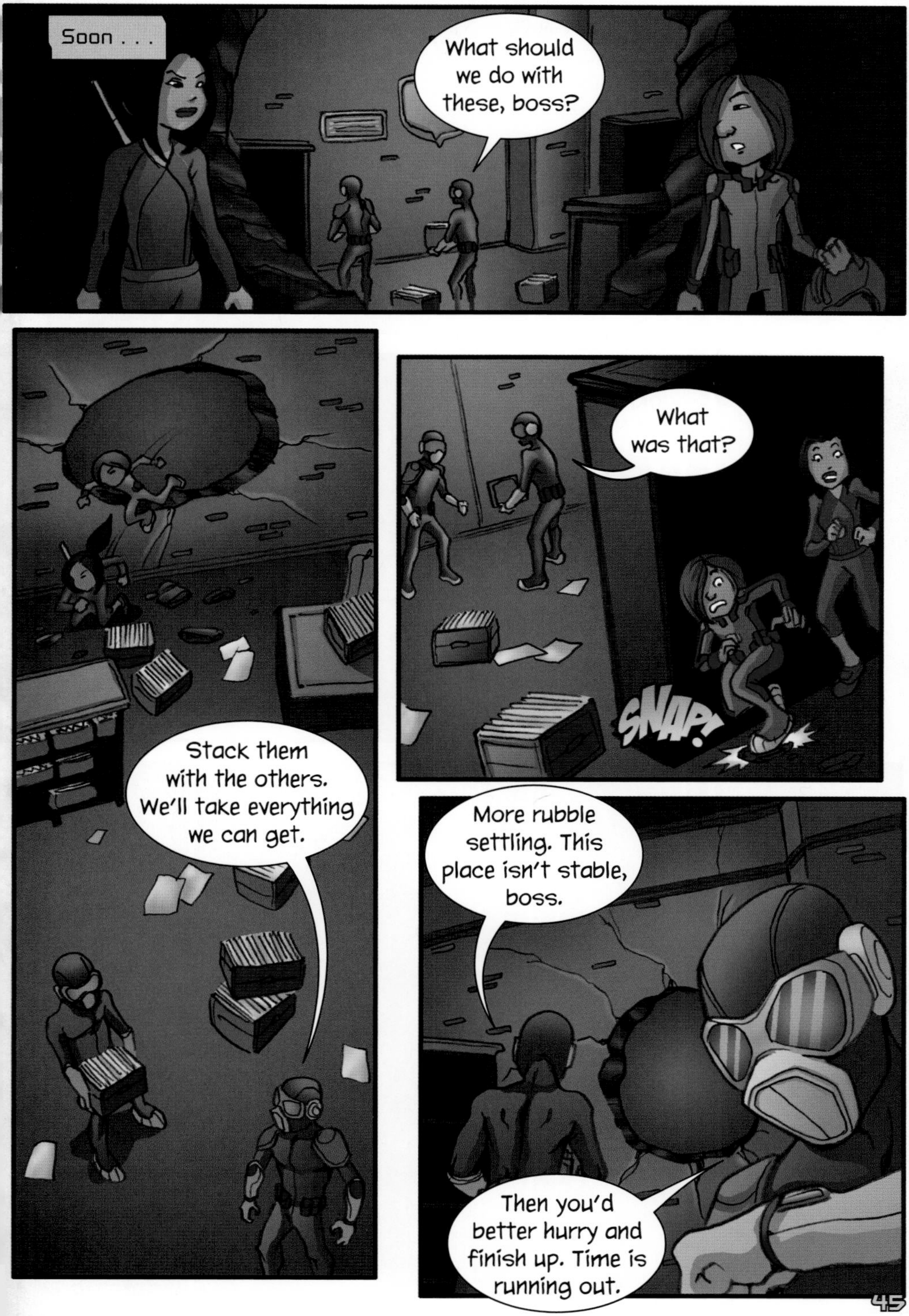

Soon . . .
What should we do with these, boss?
Stack them with the others. We'll take everything we can get.
What was that?
SNAP!
More rubble settling. This place isn't stable, boss.
Then you'd better hurry and finish up. Time is running out.

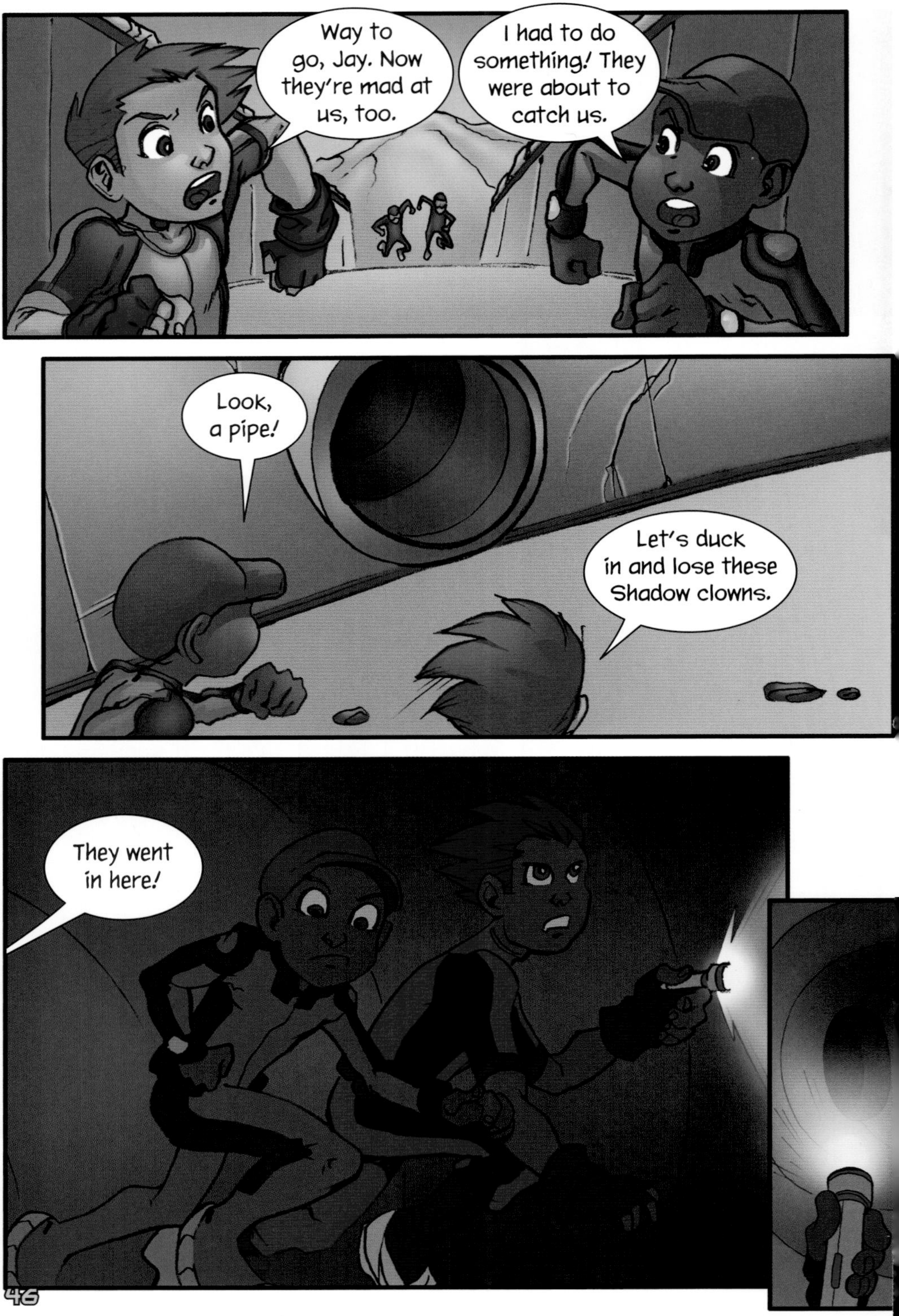
Way to go, Jay. Now they're mad at us, too.
I had to do something! They were about to catch us.
Look, a pipe!
Let's duck in and lose these Shadow clowns.
They went in here!

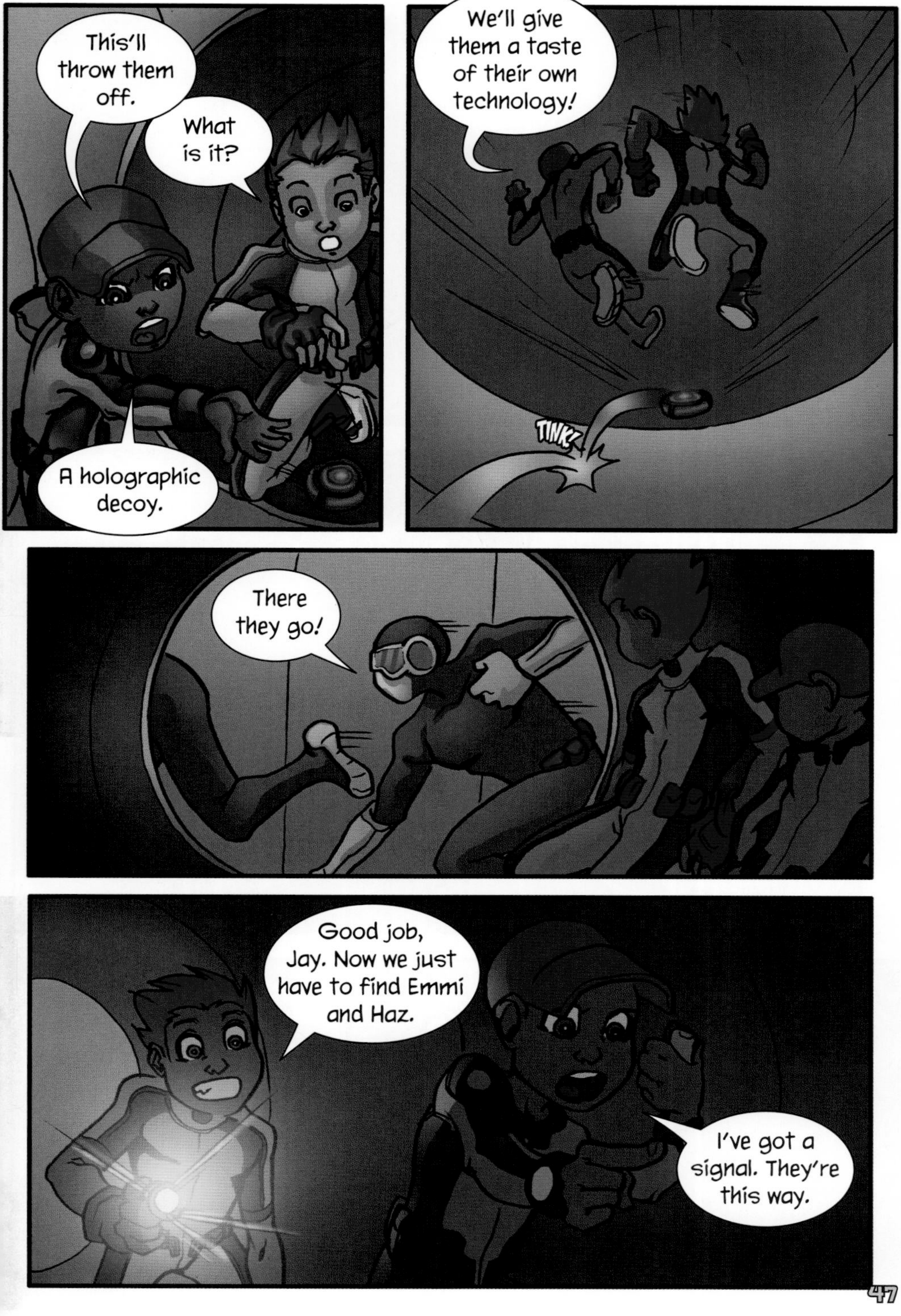
This'll throw them off.
What is it?
A holographic decoy.
We'll give them a taste of their own technology!
TINK!
There they go!
Good job, Jay. Now we just have to find Emmi and Haz.
I've got a signal. They're this way.

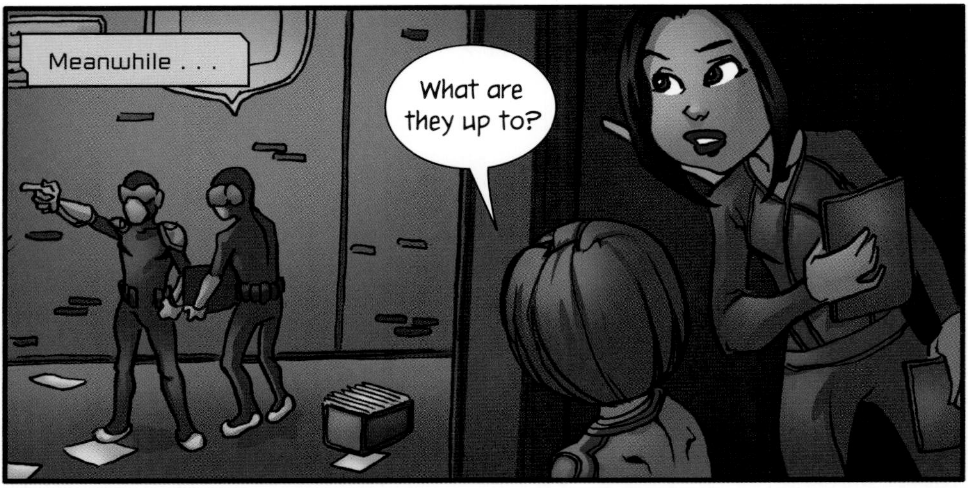
Meanwhile . . .
What are they up to?

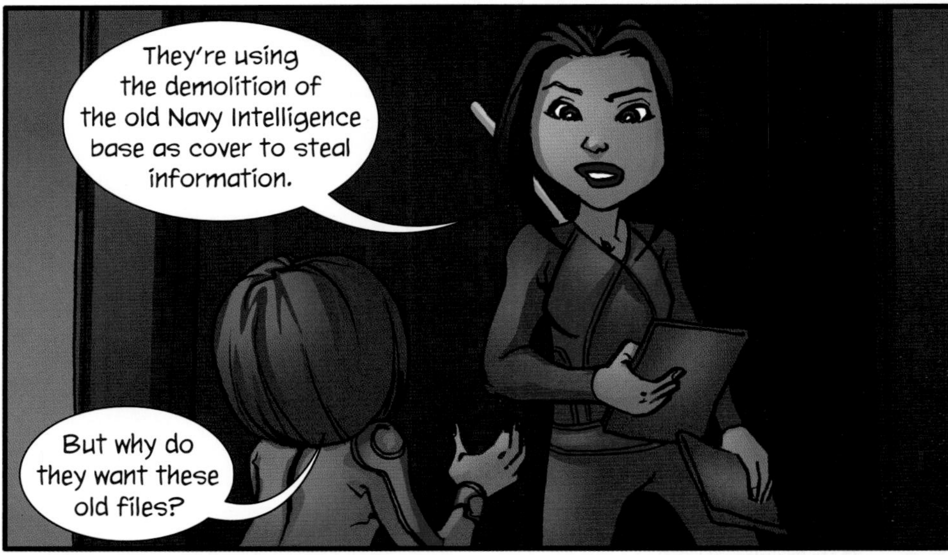
They're using the demolition of the old Navy Intelligence base as cover to steal information.
But why do they want these old files?

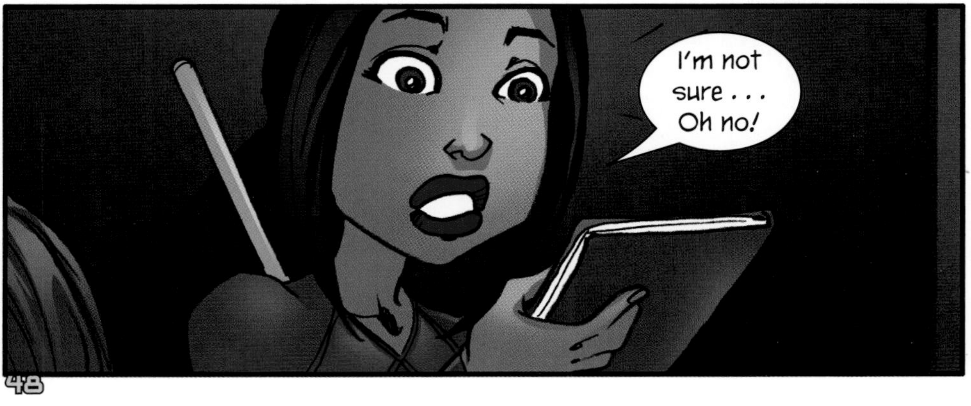
I'm not sure . . . Oh no!

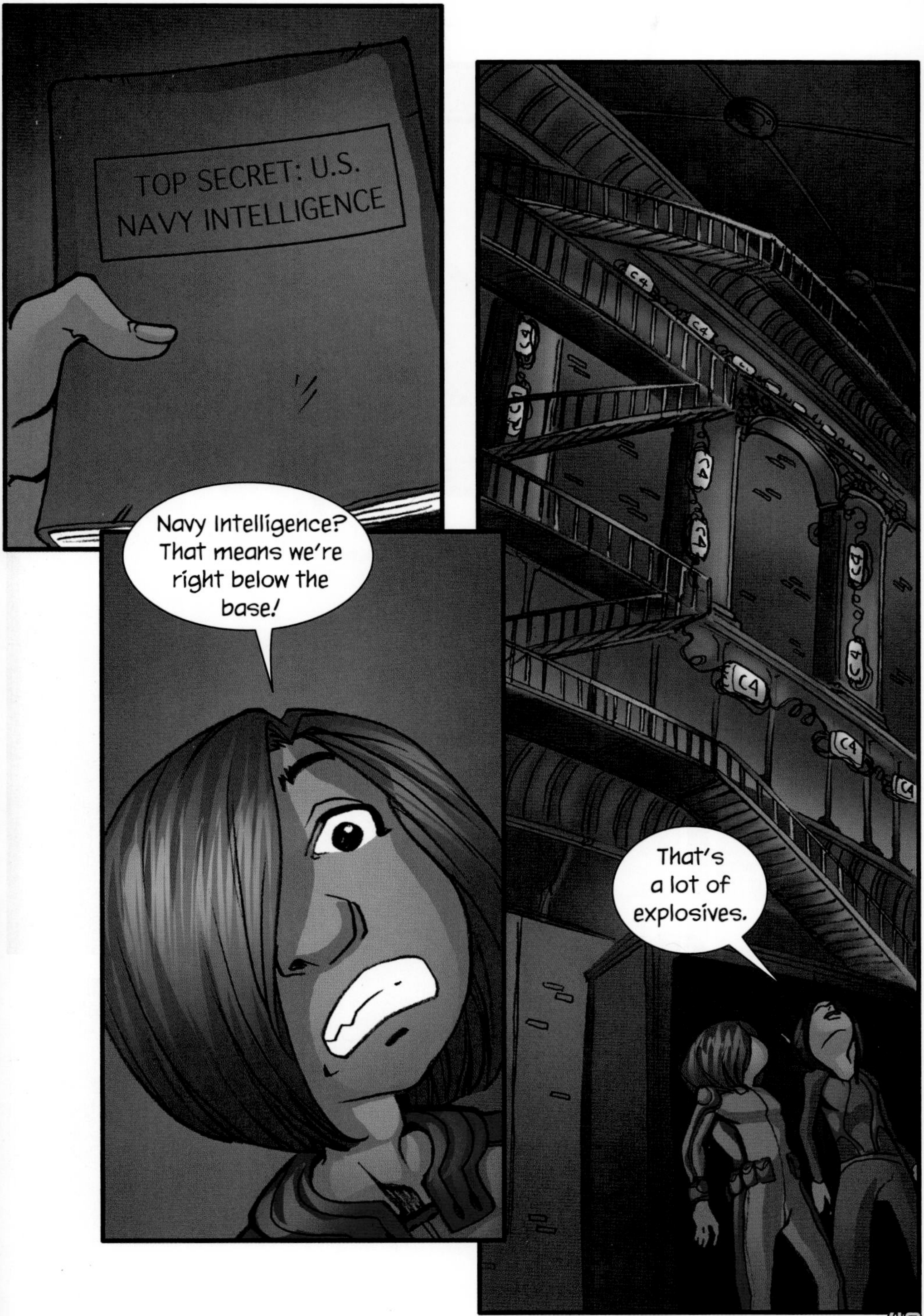
TOP SECRET: U.S. NAVY INTELLIGENCE
Navy Intelligence? That means we're right below the base!
C4
That's a lot of explosives.

SECTION

6

ACCESS GRANTED ⟫⟫

RECON ACADEMY
SECRET SECURITY FORCE

128718
293829
9283
98289
89
1
109201
192091
1992

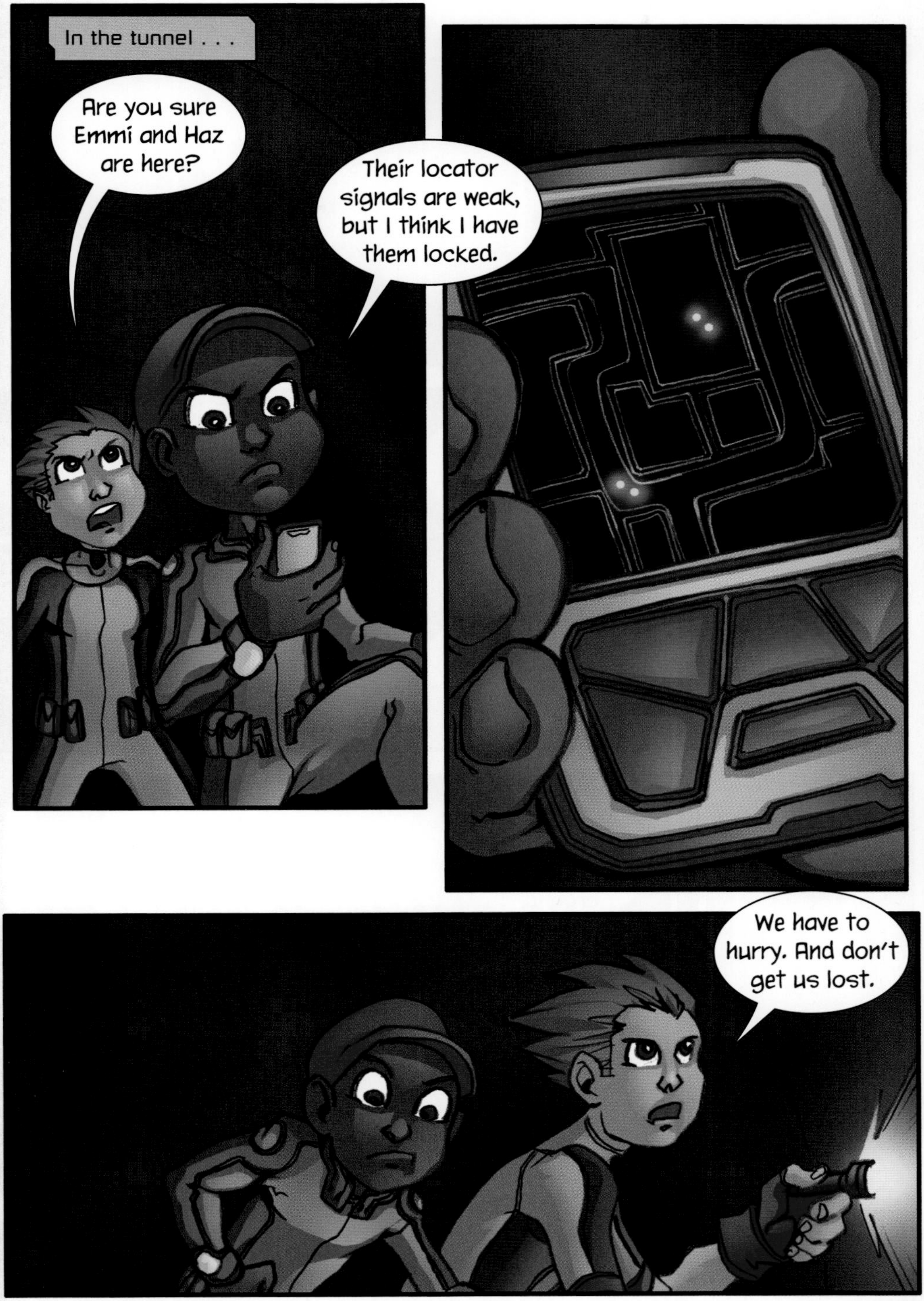
In the tunnel . . .
Are you sure Emmi and Haz are here?
Their locator signals are weak, but I think I have them locked.
We have to hurry. And don't get us lost.

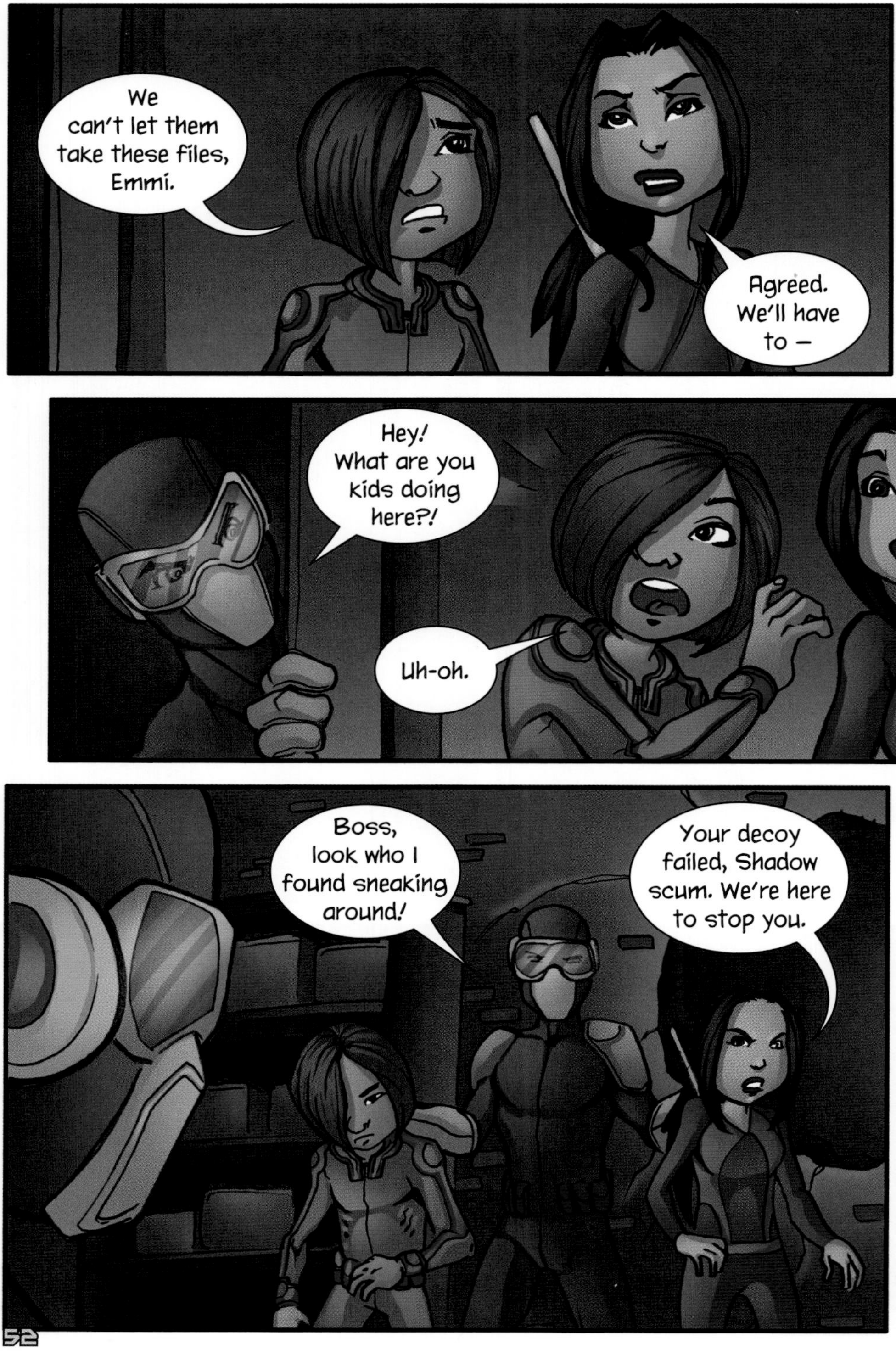
We can't let them take these files, Emmi.
Agreed. We'll have to —
Hey! What are you kids doing here?!
Uh-oh.
Boss, look who I found sneaking around!
Your decoy failed, Shadow scum. We're here to stop you.

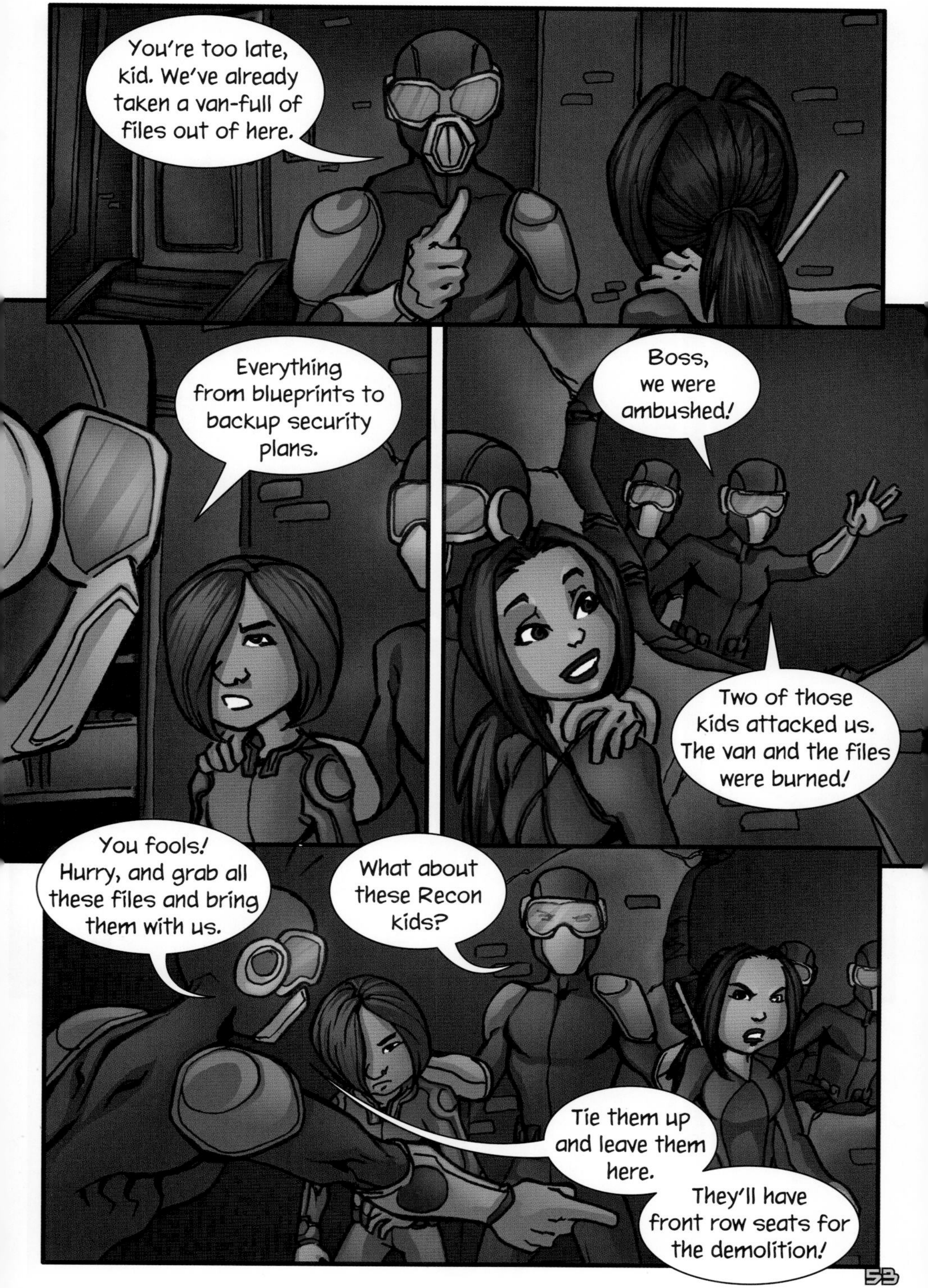
You're too late, kid. We've already taken a van-full of files out of here.
Everything from blueprints to backup security plans.
Boss, we were ambushed!
Two of those kids attacked us. The van and the files were burned!
You fools! Hurry, and grab all these files and bring them with us.
What about these Recon kids?
Tie them up and leave them here.
They'll have front row seats for the demolition!

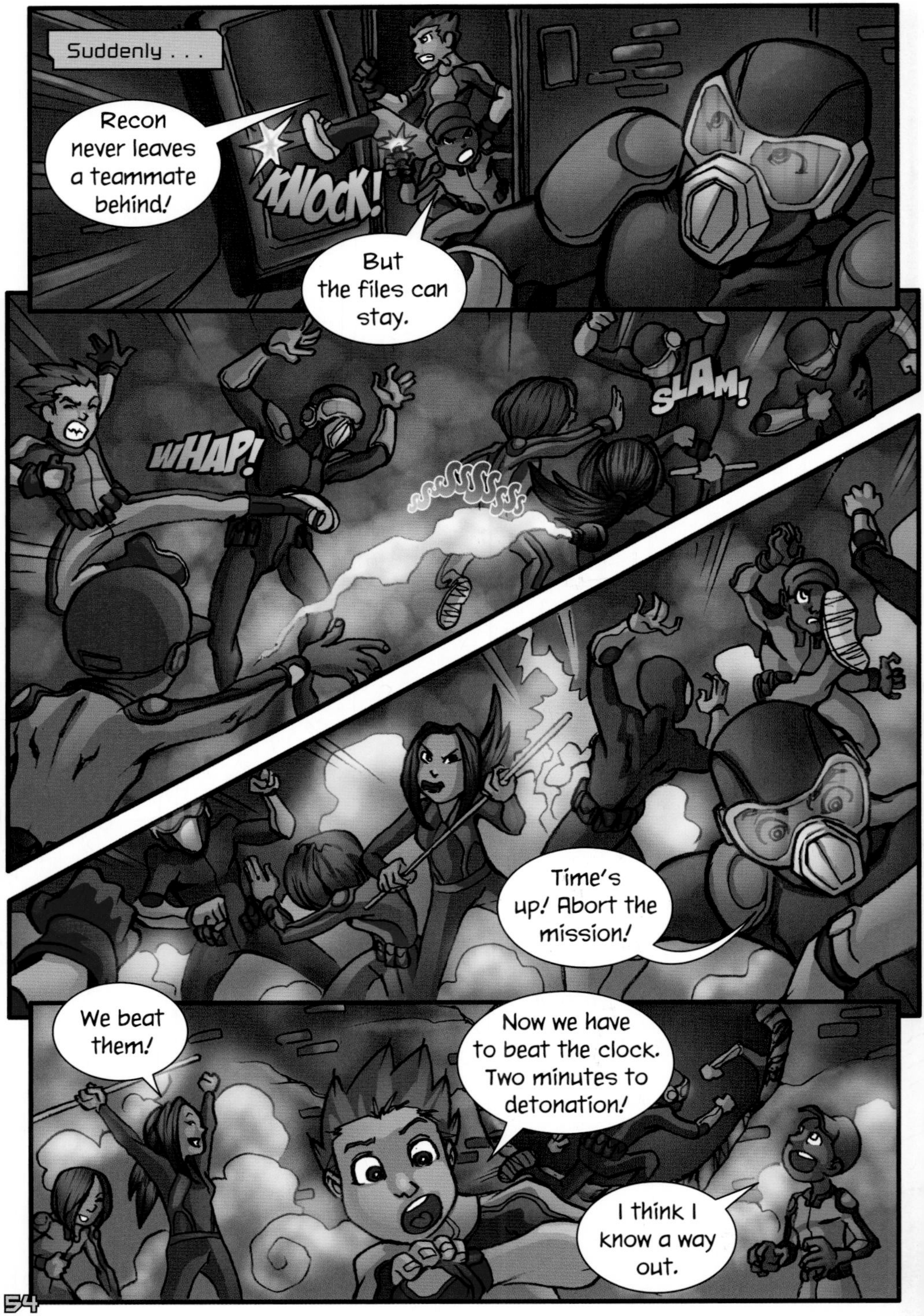
Suddenly . . .
Recon never leaves a teammate behind!
KNOCK!
But the files can stay.
WHAP!
SLAM!
SSSSSSSSS
Time's up! Abort the mission!
We beat them!
Now we have to beat the clock. Two minutes to detonation!
I think I know a way out.

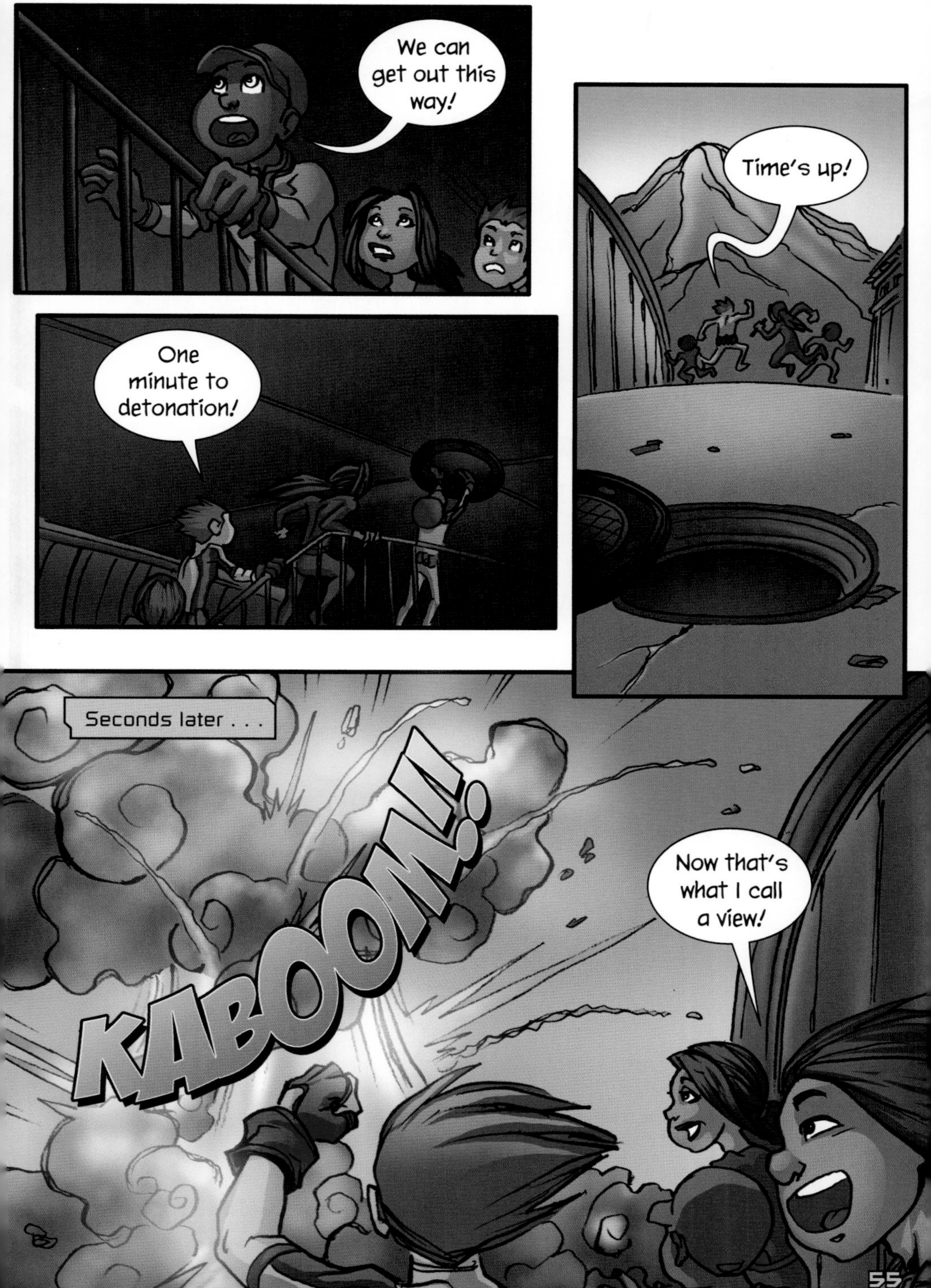
We can get out this way!
One minute to detonation!
Time's up!
Seconds later . . .
KABOOM!!!
Now that's what I call a view!

SPYSPACE
a place for international spies

CHAT ROOM PROFILES

NAME: William Ryker

AGE: 15

HEIGHT: 5' 7"

WEIGHT: 132 lbs.

EYES: Green

HAIR: Brown

SPY ORG: Recon Academy

SPECIAL ABILITIES: Technology expert, specializing in computers and communication devices

NAME: Jeremiah Johnson

AGE: 13

HEIGHT: 5' 5"

WEIGHT: 120 lbs.

EYES: Brown

HAIR: None

SPY ORG: Recon Academy

SPECIAL ABILITIES: Gadget guru and a totally gnarly skateboarder

HOME SEARCH BROWSE LOGOUT

PHOTOS

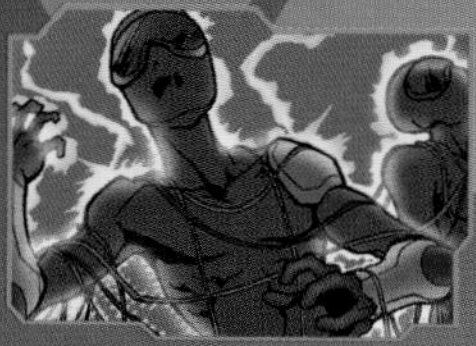

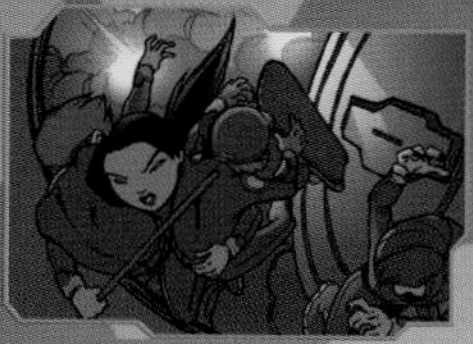

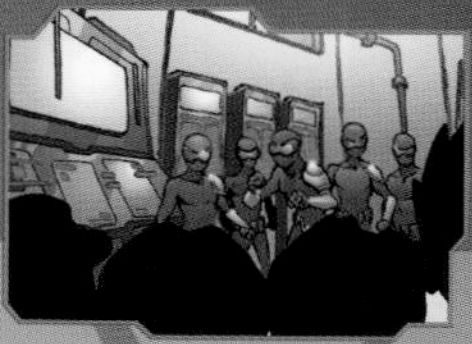

INSTANT CHAT

recent posts

see all

Hey, Jay! How's it going?

Not bad, although I still haven't gotten all of the sand out of my uniform.

Tell me about it. I don't think we've ever had an assignment that intense!

Yeah, really EXPLOSIVE!:)

I'm serious, Jay. I can't remember a more difficult mission for Recon. Still, each one of us handled their task with ease.

You know, I think we're finally all starting to grow up a little.

Jay... Jay, are you still online?

Sorry, Ryker. My mom says I have to take a bath...

Maybe I spoke too soon.

⟩ CASE FILE

CASE: "Demolition Day"
CASE NUMBER: 9781434219176
AGENTS: Ryker and Jay
ORGANIZATION: Recon Academy

SUBJECT: Demolition

OVERVIEW: Shadow Cell has intel on important government buildings scheduled for demolition. It is vital that Recon Academy oversees the demolitions so that Shadow Cell cannot apprehend classified government documents. National security is at stake.

METHODS:
Explosives
Building implosion
Wrecking balls

INTELLIGENCE:

demolition (dem-uh-LIH-shun)—the destruction, or tearing down, of buildings and structures

detonate (DET-uh-nate)—to set off an explosion

implosion (im-PLOH-zhuhn)—a violent collapse inward, or explosion from the inside

DEMOLITION METHODS:

Structures are usually pulled down using equipment like cranes and bulldozers. Larger structures, however, may require the use of more complex methods . . .

BUILDING IMPLOSION — explosives are placed on structurally important parts of buildings, and then detonated simultaneously. If done correctly, this causes the building to fall in its footprint, or straight on top of itself. The placement of these explosives is vital — if they are placed incorrectly, the structure can fall sideways and damage other buildings.

WRECKING BALL — a heavy, steel ball. Wrecking balls are particularly effective for destroying concrete and masonry. However, they are harder to control, and usually send debris flying, making the surrounding area unsafe.

The tallest structure to ever be demolished was the 47-story Singer Building in New York City. Demolitionists used building implosion to bring the structure down.

CONCLUSION:

Recon Academy has been trained in demolition safety to ensure that nothing is damaged, and no one is injured, in the process.

› ABOUT THE AUTHOR

Chris Everheart always dreamed of interesting places, fascinating people, and exciting adventures. He is still a dreamer. He enjoys writing thrilling stories about young heroes who live in a world that doesn't always understand them. Chris lives in Tennessee with his family. He plans to travel to every continent on the globe, see interesting places, meet fascinating people, and have exciting adventures.

› ABOUT THE ILLUSTRATOR

Arcana Studios, Inc. was founded by Sean O'Reilly in Coquitlam, British Columbia, in 2004. Four years later, Arcana has established itself as Canada's largest comic book and graphic novel publisher with over 100 comics and 9 books released. A nomination for a Harvey Award and winning the "Schuster Award for Top Publisher" are just a few of Arcana's accolades. The studio is known as a quality publisher for independent comic books and graphic novels.

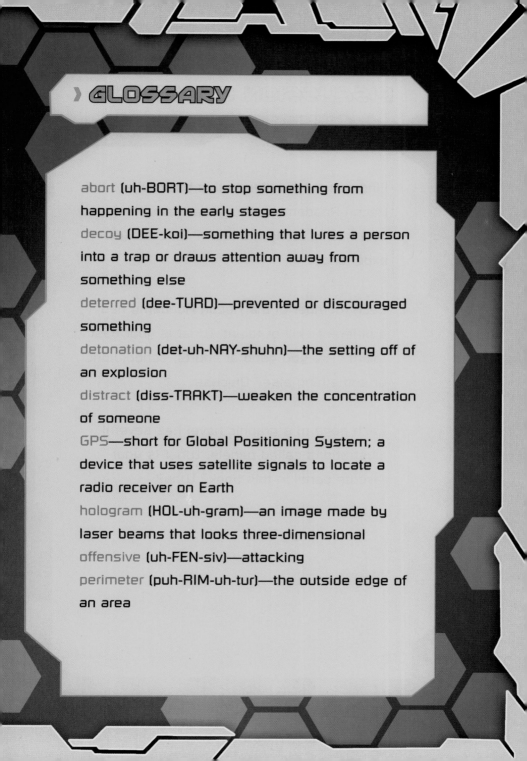

GLOSSARY

abort (uh-BORT)—to stop something from happening in the early stages

decoy (DEE-koi)—something that lures a person into a trap or draws attention away from something else

deterred (dee-TURD)—prevented or discouraged something

detonation (det-uh-NAY-shuhn)—the setting off of an explosion

distract (diss-TRAKT)—weaken the concentration of someone

GPS—short for Global Positioning System; a device that uses satellite signals to locate a radio receiver on Earth

hologram (HOL-uh-gram)—an image made by laser beams that looks three-dimensional

offensive (uh-FEN-siv)—attacking

perimeter (puh-RIM-uh-tur)—the outside edge of an area

❯ DISCUSSION QUESTIONS

1. Find some examples in this book where the Recon Academy works as a team. Have you ever had to work in a team? Discuss your experience.

2. Each member of the Recon Academy has a different skill or talent. What is your best talent? Are you good at sports, schoolwork, or something else? Discuss.

3. Each page of a graphic novel has several illustrations called panels. What is your favorite panel in this book? Why?

1. The Recon Academy has four members. Create a fifth member of the Recon Team. What is he or she like? What type of skills does this new member bring to the team?

2. Write your own Recon Academy story. What problems will the Recon Team face? Will they succeed or fail? You decide.

3. Many comic books are written and illustrated by two different people. Write a story, and then give it to a friend to illustrate.